AMBUSH RECKONING

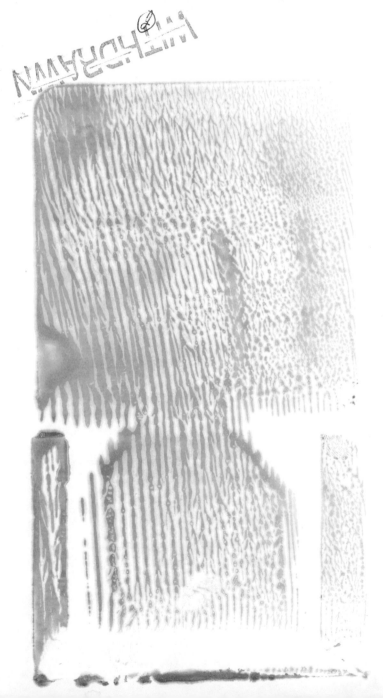

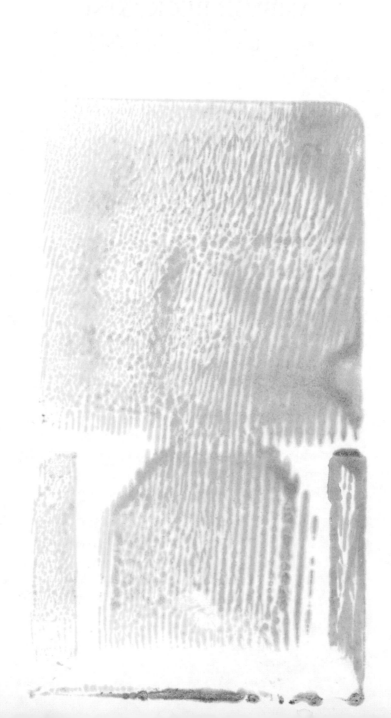

AMBUSH RECKONING

D. B. Newton

Chivers Press • G.K. Hall & Co.
Bath, England • Thorndike, Maine USA

This Large Print edition is published by Chivers Press, England, and by G.K. Hall & Co., USA.

Published in 1998 in the U.K. by arrangement with Golden West Literary Agency.

Published in 1998 in the U.S. by arrangement with Golden West Literary Agency.

U.K. Hardcover ISBN 0–7540–3289–2 (Chivers Large Print)
U.K. Softcover   ISBN 0–7540–3290–6 (Camden Large Print)
U.S. Softcover   ISBN 0–7838–8455–9 (Nightingale Series Edition)

The text of this Large Print edition is unabridged.
Other aspects of the book may vary from the original edition.

Set in 16 pt. New Times Roman.

Printed in Great Britain on acid-free paper.

British Library Cataloguing in Publication Data available

Library of Congress Cataloging-in-Publication Data

Newton, D. B. (Dwight Bennett), 1916-
    Ambush reckoning / D. B. Newton.
    p. (large print)   cm.
    ISBN 0-7838-8455-9 (lg. print : sc : alk. paper)
    1. Large type books.   I. Title.
    [PS3527.E9178A8   1998]
    813'.52—dc21   98-10490

CHAPTER ONE

A harvest moon, the size of a bushel basket, had broken above the timbered crests by the time the lamps of Reserve showed ahead. In this golden spill of light Troy Holden tried to make out the expression on the man in the other saddle. A continuing silence, throughout the length of their ride, had held the weight of stern disapproval; Holden felt the pressure more than he cared to admit. At last he was stung to speech.

'I know what you're thinking. So, you might as well put it into words!'

Sam Riggs stared straight ahead, past his horse's ears, at the swimming lights of the nearing cattle town. His voice was stiff with reproach. 'Would it do any good?'

'If you mean, will it change my decision any—I'm afraid not.' Holden spoke as bluntly as his foreman. 'I know how you feel. But, you could try at least to understand my problem. I've told you, I wouldn't be doing this if there was any other way.'

'Yeah—you told me.' The older man gave a shrug. 'Hell—I guess I know! Crown means nothing to you. It never really did.'

'That isn't so!'

'Near enough! I don't figure you've lost any sleep over what you're doing. I know damn well

1

it's nothing Vern Holden could ever have done.' He added bitterly: 'But, you ain't Vern.'

Troy Holden nodded. 'That's right,' he said curtly, 'I'm not my father. And I'm afraid there's nothing you can do about it.'

Sam Riggs said, in the same harsh tone, 'That's why I been keeping my mouth shut!'

That effectively killed the talk between them. Also, by now, the wagon ruts made a turn, picked up a first fringe of houses, and became the main street of the village. They rode in without hurry. Tang of dust, and the smoke of evening fires, mingled with the smells of sun-cured grass and pine left over from the short fall day. Lamplight in windows seemed pale against the golden glow of the round moon that hung above the street, laying shadows as black and straight as if they had been first drawn with a ruler and then generously inked in.

It was early enough that most of the stores were still open, while Reserve's two saloons were brightly lighted but not yet doing the usual Friday night's business. In front of the station, a stage was making up for its run to meet the railroad. The coach lamps were lit and the four-horse team stood restless in harness, while the station agent busied himself storing luggage into the rear boot.

Troy Holden reined in and, from the saddle, spoke to the agent. 'Have I got time to mail a letter?'

2

Melcher, postmaster as well as the stage line's agent in Reserve, peered up at him—a harried-looking man, wearing a green eyeshade and black alpaca sleeve protectors. 'You're just under the wire, Mr. Holden. I was all ready to lock the pouch and toss it aboard.'

'I'd appreciate getting this into it.' Holden handed down an envelope he'd taken from his pocket. One eyebrow quirked as the man hefted the bulkiness of several sheets of letter paper. Holden saw him glance at the inscription—to a Miss Beatrice Applegate, of New York City.

Holden said, 'I was wondering if you happen to have any mail for Crown in the office?'

'Why, no, Mr. Holden. Not since your rider picked up the last batch on Tuesday.'

'You're very sure? No chance it could have been overlooked?'

Melcher was positive. 'No chance at all. Why? Are you missing something? It might be in tomorrow,' he suggested helpfully. 'When this coach finishes its run to the railroad and back . . .'

'Thanks,' Holden said. 'I'll check later.' From Melcher's knowing look Holden understood the agent had guessed it was an overdue letter from a girl that had him so concerned. Not greatly caring, he rode on with Sam Riggs, still silent and hostile, flanking him.

At the end of the block, beyond an intersection, stood the hotel—Reserve's largest

3

structure, a graceless, two-story box of a building; catty-cornered from it a lantern burned at the entrance to the public livery. Here, a hunch-shouldered old man who served as night hostler came down the ramp as the two riders stepped off, into dust that had been beaten to flour by countless hooves, and took the reins and the silver dollar Holden tossed him.

Occupied with his own thoughts, Holden turned away without even hearing the old man's respectful greeting; but Riggs paused to exchange a word or two, before hurrying to overtake his employer as he took the wide street crossing toward the hotel. An observer would have found almost nothing in common between these two. The foreman was a rawboned, sunburned man whose rugged features matched his range clothes and sweat-rimmed hat, and the boots whose leather had long since shaped into iron-hard and comfortable creases. By contrast, the owner of Crown ranch—some twenty years his junior—had the mark of a different world on him.

It showed in the careful cut of whipcord jacket and riding pants, in the benchmade boots with the highlight that ran across the polished surface as he mounted the veranda steps and walked inside the hotel. Troy Holden looked out of place against the faded rawness of a cowtown hotel lobby; he was aware of it, and he would have said it made no slightest

4

difference to him—this was not his world and he had no intention of remaining long enough for it to touch him in any way.

Across the dingy room, with its worn carpeting and sagging furniture and its single dusty rubber tree in a pot, the proprietor and his wife were discussing some matter of business. Holden went over and laid a hand on the edge of the desk. 'George Lunceford,' he said.

They looked at him, and each other. Sid Bravender was short and going to paunch and baldness; his wife, built on a more heroic scale, held an armload of sheets and blankets folded beneath the full shelf of her heavy bosom. The hotel keeper cleared his throat. 'I believe he's checked out, Mr. Holden.'

The latter frowned, aware of Sam Riggs moving up beside him. 'Checked out? That hardly seems possible.'

'I was on the desk,' the woman said. 'Not half an hour ago. He said something about taking the night stage. I don't know if he's actually left his room yet.'

Holden, too astonished to answer, heard Sam Riggs' grunt and felt the man's touch on his arm. He swung away from the desk, toward the stairs leading from the second floor.

They creaked faintly as a man descended— first only his legs visible, and a hand carrying a carpetbag; then the faint gleam of a gold watchchain stretched across the waistcoat of his business suit. The rest of the man came in view. He was pink-faced, clean shaven, except for thick muttonchops that were frosted with gray. When he saw Holden, below him in the lobby, he halted abruptly as though he half considered turning back.

'Ah—Holden,' he said, in a tone of transparent discomfort. 'Good evening to you.'

'I *thought* it was a good evening,' Troy Holden answered shortly, unable to keep the anger from his voice. He nodded toward the hotel keeper and his wife. 'These people tell me you're leaving. If I hadn't come early, appears I almost might even have missed you.'

George Lunceford came the rest of the way down the steps, still clutching his carpetbag. His eyes slid uneasily from Holden to Sam Riggs and back again. He tried a smile. 'I'm sorry. It's something that came up suddenly. Unavoidable. A telegram . . .' He was sidestepping as he spoke, edging toward the open street door.

'You couldn't at least have got word to me?'

'There really wasn't time. You know how it is in business.' Sweat was shining on the smooth cheeks; the smile became a painful grimace. 'I'm afraid you'll have to excuse me now—really. The stage—'

'Just a minute!' Holden was having trouble keeping his voice under control. He flung an irritated look at the unwelcome witnesses to his private business, but the Bravenders stood

6

rooted, listening with unconcealed curiosity. With a lift of the shoulders, Troy Holden turned back to the businessman.

'I don't have to like this! I've spent three days of a tight schedule, showing you my ranch. I've answered every question you could raise. We agreed I was to meet you tonight and settle on terms. Just what becomes of all that?'

Lunceford swallowed. A tic had begun to pluck at a nerve in his cheek. 'I've told you I'm sorry. But in business one can never be certain. Things change in an hour...'

'Then you are *not* buying? If that's what you mean, why can't you come out and say it?'

A voice spoke from the street door, carrying a freight of harsh amusement. 'That stage is ready to roll. Friend Lunceford don't want to miss it...'

Holden saw panic break across the face of the man before him. Slowly, he turned.

The one who leaned in the doorway had both thumbs hooked in a heavy shellbelt that dragged at his middle. Untrimmed, rusty-looking hair showed beneath a shapeless hat. The eyes, above slanting cheekbones, were a pale and piercing blue; the full lips held a perpetual sneer. Everything about him hinted of a wild and feral danger.

He spoke again, into the silence. 'They won't hold that stage, you know—even if you have bought your ticket. You better run along, little man...'

7

A sound broke from George Lunceford. Suddenly, without another look at Troy Holden, he was heading toward the door. The redhead made no slightest effort to give room and Lunceford was forced to sidle past, sucking in his middle as though terrified at the idea of their touching. By the time he crossed the veranda and hit the dry plankings of the boardwalk below he was already breaking into a run. The hurried sounds quickly faded.

Holden drew a breath to settle the anger that left him trembling. His stare met the pale eyes of the man in the doorway. 'I take it this was your doing,' he said into the heavy stillness. 'I don't think I know you.'

The thick lips quirked; the sneer became more pronounced. 'Don't you?'

Sam Riggs spoke hastily. 'His name's Seab Glazer. He rides with Bartell's crowd . . .'

Glazer suggested, with bland amusement, 'You've heard of *him*, maybe?'

'Luke Bartell? The cattle rustler? The man that runs a traffic in stolen beef and horses, back and forth across the Canadian border?'

'Is that what Sam told you?' The pale eyes narrowed a trifle, as they cut to the foreman's scowling face. 'Why, now, you shouldn't listen to talk, Holden. Some people don't care what they say.'

'It's common knowledge!' the foreman retorted.

'It's never been proved. Not in a court of

8

law.'

'Law courts are pretty far between, out here.' But having said that, Riggs appeared to lose some of his aggressiveness. Looking at him, Troy Holden guessed that the Crown foreman was beginning to feel the full weight of threat from the man in the doorway. Meanwhile both Bravenders, yonder by the desk, were watching with the shocked expressions of people afraid to move or almost to breathe. He didn't need any stronger hints that he faced a real danger.

But Holden was too furious at the moment to weigh precautions. He told Seab Glazer, coldly, 'I'm not concerned with who Bartell is, or how he spends his time. I want to know if it was his orders that you should go to work and run George Lunceford out of town—just when we were about to close a deal.'

Glazer countered with an amused question. 'And, supposing it was?'

'Do you think I'm going to stand tamely by and let him interfere in my business—whatever his reasons?'

The pale eyes studied him, insolently noting the lack of gun or holster, the well-tailored Eastern clothing, the smooth features that showed no mark of sun or elements. Seab Glazer let him have that mocking half-smile.

'You talk real good,' he said with a sneer. 'I'd like to hear how well you say some of that to Luke, himself. So happens he's gonna be in

9

town, later tonight—over at the Montana House. I think he'd get quite a kick out of it!'

The sound of a four-horse team breaking into a gallop, of creaking leather and slamming timbers and rolling iron, suddenly was born in the street outside and went sweeping past the hotel. Through the door Troy Holden had a quick glimpse of the stagecoach, its lamps gleaming; then it was gone and a fog of dust was settling. Seab Glazer had turned his head to watch the stage go past. When he swung back again he was grinning wickedly, showing a glint of strong white teeth.

'Well, your friend Lunceford made the stage,' he remarked pleasantly enough. 'That's good. I wouldn't have wanted to worry about him.' He straightened then, lazily, pushing away from the doorframe with an easy movement. As he did his arm dropped, the fingers of his right hand carelessly brushing the handle of the holstered gun. Holden sensed the way Sam Riggs, at his side, stiffened and caught his breath.

But Glazer didn't pull the gun. Instead he raised his hand and adjusted the set of his shapeless, sweat-marked Stetson, smoothed back the unshorn rusty hair that hung raggedly almost to his collar. 'Guess I'll be getting on over to the Montana House,' he said, still grinning, 'to wait for Luke. I'll tell him you may be dropping by—all right?' Not waiting for an answer he deliberately turned his back and, with a clink of spurs, vanished into the darkness.

CHAPTER TWO

A muffled exclamation from Sam Riggs broke the lobby's stillness. Troy Holden scarcely noticed. Anger drove him forward in the wake of the redhead; he strode directly after him, through the open door and onto the hotel veranda.

Halting at the rail, he watched Glazer move at an angle across the moonwashed street, toward the lights of the Montana House. The man skirted a pair of horses at the tie rail, mounted to the boardwalk and walked inside the saloon.

A step sounded, and Sam Riggs loomed next to Holden in the half-shadow and half-moonlight of the hotel porch. Riggs said harshly, 'What the hell do you make of *that*?'

Holden found that his hands were gripping the rail until the splintered wood scored his palms. He straightened, drawing a deep breath. 'I was just about to ask you! This Luke Bartell: He's really as tough as I've been hearing?'

Sam Riggs spat across the rail, into the weed-grown dirt. 'He's a bad one! The past couple years since he and his gang first showed up in this western Montana country, they've

11

done just about what they please. Rustling's their specialty, though they don't stop with that. Bartell himself has killed three men, that I know about.'

'And he's allowed to get away with it? I'm to believe that he can ride openly into a place like this—even send a man ahead to announce him, and run George Lunceford out of town—and nothing at all is done?'

He caught the bitter, nearly scornful look that Riggs shot him. 'Trouble with you, you think you're still in New York City,' the foreman said. 'You think all you got to do is holler for a policeman. Out here, things just ain't that simple.'

'You're still under the law,' Holden reminded him, but Riggs only shrugged.

'You've seen our law! Poor old Peters is a good enough fellow to have a drink with, but as a sheriff's deputy he don't draw a hell of a lot of water. And as far as the sheriff himself is concerned, this is a remote end of a big country. Not many votes here—a lot easier for him to close his ears to any rumors of things that go on.'

'There must be more than rumors! Have you no hard evidence—no witnesses to force the sheriff to act, whether he wants to or not?'

Riggs impatiently shook his head. 'I tell you, you just don't understand. It would take an army to handle Bartell's crowd, and there ain't that much money in the county treasury. And so, who's going to offer himself up as a witness, for Bartell to take care of in his own good time? No, Holden—if you stayed around you'd learn a man here has to pack his own law, in his own holster. And he leaves it there and minds his business, except when somebody forces his hand.'

Scowling, Troy Holden asked, 'What about Crown, in all this? Perhaps these outlaws have been making us trouble, that you've conveniently forgotten to tell me about . . .'

'No!' the foreman answered stiffly, and Holden knew he had succeeded in making him angry. 'If it had been so, I'd of told you. The fact is, Bartell has left all the valley ranches pretty much alone. It's one of the reasons he knows he can come and go, just about as he likes. A man has plenty to keep him busy with his own affairs, as long as his toes aren't stepped on.'

'Mine are being stepped on,' Troy Holden pointed out. 'And hard! By this time I ought to have had the papers signed, and a check for Crown in my pocket. For reasons I can't begin to fathom, Bartell decided to sic his redheaded gunman on Lunceford and ruin the deal for me. I may have to do what Glazer said: If Bartell's really going to be at the Montana House, it looks as though there's no choice but to find out from him what he thinks he's up to.'

The foreman's head jerked around, his eyes searching Holden's face in the dim light. 'You

13

ain't talking about trying to brace Luke Bartell! Man, use your head! He'll have his whole bunch with him—and there's only the two of us here, from Crown. They could eat us alive!'

It was Troy Holden's turn to stare. Riggs' tacit assumption of a share in any trouble involving the brand he rode for showed a loyalty that was new in Holden's experience. Frowning, he shook his head as he answered shortly, 'I'm not going to get eaten alive, and I don't ask anyone else to. Not for a few acres of grass and a few hundred head of cattle. But I *do* intend to get my price out of that ranch—I don't care who tries to interfere, or for whatever reason.'

'So we're back where we started!' Riggs' voice sounded heavy with resignation. 'You still mean to sell. I was almost beginning to hope you might be mad enough—'

Holden cut him off. 'I can't help what you may have hoped. You know my reasons for selling. I realize you put a good many years into Crown, as my father's manager and even before that; I can see you probably feel you almost own the place . . .'

'I never said that!' Riggs exclaimed. 'But it's a fine ranch—or it could be, if it'd ever been developed the way it should. Only, the kind you intend selling to—like that Lunceford dude! Hell, I heard some of the darn fool questions he asked! What does a man like that know? Why, he'll ruin it!' Sam Riggs spoke with

14

heartfelt earnestness. 'Your pa had him a dream. As it happened he never got to work it out; but I knew his plans for Crown, and they were good ones. If you could somehow just change your mind—'

'We've said all this before,' Troy Holden broke in. 'Nothing's changed except that I've lost time I couldn't afford, thinking I was going to do business with Lunceford. Well, there are other buyers—but I can't risk any more delays.

'I'll get some telegrams written. I want them run over to the railroad, first thing in the morning. You'll either have to send one of the hands, or take them yourself.'

The foreman's shoulders settled within his brush jacket; some of the spirit seemed to go out of him. He lifted a rope-gnarled hand, and let it drop again. 'Sure,' he said in heavy resignation. 'You write your telegrams, Holden. Me—I think maybe I'm gonna go get drunk!'

Not waiting to be dismissed, he swung away and tramped down the plank steps, and strode off through the heavy golden moonlight. Troy Holden swore to himself. Afterward, with a shake of his head, he turned and walked again into the hotel lobby.

He ignored Sid Bravender's open stare as he crossed the worn linoleum to a writing table, in a corner near the tired-looking rubber plant. Seating himself, he looked for writing materials but there were none in the desk's pigeonholes;

instead he found an old envelope in his pocket and, uncapping his reservoir pen, settled to drafting a telegram.

As he worked he was already drawing up in his mind a list of prospects—men or firms that controlled the means to buy in a property like Crown ranch. But after some moments, his pen slowed, and halted. Frowning, he looked at what he had written. With an angry gesture he crumpled the envelope into a ball, and fired it at the wastebasket by the table.

Until this puzzling situation involving Luke Bartell was explained and somehow resolved, everything connected with Crown was left hanging and in doubt. The more he thought about it, the more clearly it came home to him that his hands were tied.

Troy Holden capped and pocketed his pen, took his narrow-brimmed hat from the table and walked out of the hotel, frustration giving a reaching length to his stride and a hard definiteness to his footsteps on the uneven sidewalk. The moon was higher now, beginning to lose its ruddy glow and turning to a frosty silver. A wind was rising, to pluck at a man's clothing and comb the street with an occasional gout of gritty dust; it brought the chill and the tang of the high timber.

The evening was tuning up. Riders passed Holden, coming in off the trails; more saddled horses stood here and there at the hitch racks. He shouldered his way past spurred and booted men upon the walk, too occupied with his own thoughts to give much attention to any of them, or to the increasing sound and activity behind the lighted windows of the town.

A man stood alone beside a wooden arcade support, half-visible in the shadow of the tin roof. Holden went past and then, as the image of the man registered with him, he paused and came around again. Halting beside the lath-lean figure that towered almost half a head above him, he said, 'Peters?'

'Mr. Holden.'

Byron Peters, the deputy sheriff for this end of a sprawling county, was a polite-spoken man; he had a way of taking his hat off and holding it against his chest when he talked to anyone, as though to diminish the added height a steeple-crowned Stetson gave his gaunt shape. 'Anything I can do for you?'

Moonlight showed the lawman's face—a good enough face except for a rather weak chin that spoiled it, and the sag of middle age. By Peters possessed a certain vague dignity, spoiled by the smell of brandy hung about him like an aura. Facing this man, Troy Holden said, 'What do you think, Sheriff? Does it look to you like a quiet evening?'

The tall man peered at the night, and the activity of the town. 'Why, yes. Seems normal for a Friday, with fall gather still a couple weeks off.'

'I wonder if you knew there's a man named

17

Seab Glazer in town—over there in the Montana House.'

In his present sour mood, it gave him a kind of satisfaction to see the startled way the bony head swung about for a look in that direction. There was a faint catch of breath in the tall man's chest before he answered, carefully, 'I can't say I keep track of everyone who rides in . . .'

'Still, it might interest you,' Holden said, 'that according to him, Luke Bartell's expected before the night's over. Probably with his whole crew.'

'Glazer said this?' By Peters digested the news, and it was obvious that it troubled him. But after a moment he suggested a trifle lamely, 'I imagine it'll be all right. They're a tough outfit, but we've never had any trouble. They walk a pretty narrow line here in Reserve.'

'Oh?' Holden felt his temper slipping. 'Perhaps you hadn't heard that Seab Glazer terrorized a man this evening—a man named Lunceford, visiting in town on honest business—and ran him out on the night stage!'

'That—that's a serious charge, Mr. Holden!'

'It happens to be true! I was there!'

'I see . . .' The lawman seemed completely taken aback. A hand crept up and fumbled at his shirtcollar. In a hoarse voice he suggested, 'It still might be hard to prove, even with witnesses. A court could say that this man

18

Lunceford simply mistook Glazer's intentions. Do you know if he intends to press the case?'

'How could he?' Holden retorted. 'I told you he'd left town!' Suddenly the futility of it overwhelmed him—the indignity of standing here trying to argue legalities with a man who walked in a perpetual fog of genteel booziness. Troy Holden lifted his shoulders.

'Forget it!' he said harshly. 'Forget I said a thing. I never did understand you people—but, it's your town, and your country; and I guess you like it the way it is. But I'm damned if I have to!'

The tall man bobbed his head. He sounded hurt. 'Now, Mr. Holden! Wait!'

'Good night!' Troy Holden said bluntly. He turned and deliberately walked away, not waiting to hear any more.

CHAPTER THREE

Before he had gone a short half block he had fairly well worked off his head of steam; but when he stopped in the faint glow of a restaurant's plate glass window, to fish up a box of tailor-made cigarettes from his coat pocket, he found his hand was still trembling slightly. He analyzed what he was feeling and decided it was very near to shame.

There was nothing to be proud of in bullying

19

an ineffectual but well-meaning man, who had probably never asked for his job but had held it all these years because no one else wanted it. At best the pay would keep By Peters in cigars and brandy and give him walking-around money, and keep him from being a financial burden on his brother's family. Holden chose his smoke, thumbed a wooden match to life and fired up. The glow of the flame, shielded by cupped palms, was on his face when he heard his name spoken, uncertainly. 'Troy? Is that you?'

He shook out the match and dropped it, turning. The girl had halted with her hand on the restaurant door-latch, about to open it when she saw him. She dropped her hand now and turned as he walked over, touching the brim of his hat to her. Callie Peters said, 'I was wondering if you'd seen my father yet this evening? Or Jim Ells?'

'No, I haven't,' he told her. 'I only got in a few minutes ago, myself.' He thought dryly that he could have added, *I was giving your Uncle By a hard time a minute ago.* He was just as glad she didn't have to know about that.

She was saying: 'I've been in town since afternoon; Pa and Jim were supposed to meet me and have supper. I'm tired waiting for them—I'm getting hungry!'

Troy Holden smiled a little. He suggested, 'Will I do as a substitute?'

That brought up a quick gasp, and then an

embarrassed laugh. 'Oh, my goodness!' she exclaimed. 'I really wasn't fishing for an invitation! But I'd like it very much.'

'Come along then,' he said, taking her elbow, and he opened the door for them both.

The diner was about half filled, the stools at the counter and a couple of the tables with their red-checkered cloths already occupied. Troy Holden found a table at the rear of the room, seated Callie and hung his narrow-brimmed hat on a nail before he took the chair across from her. He listened, amused, as she exchanged greetings with the proprietor, a fat man with an apron tied under his armpits. She ordered solidly—steak and potatoes and the trimmings.

Holden liked Callie Peters, whose full name—Calpurnia—must have been discovered by her mother in some battered copy of Shakespeare's *Julius Caesar*. Actually he had known her a long time. All the Peters family ran to tallness, and she already had her height when he first met her. She'd lost that early, awkward coltishness, had filled out and turned into a sunny-haired, attractive young woman; but she could never disguise the fact that she was and would always be a creature of the cattle ranges, without polish or social graces.

The man in the apron joshed a moment with the girl and then looked at Holden. Holden said, 'I think I'll just have some coffee. I find I'm not really hungry.'

Alone, Callie looked at him anxiously. 'Is anything wrong?'

'Nothing,' he said quickly, but he was afraid she wasn't reassured. For a quietness descended upon her and they said little during the next few moments while Holden finished his cigarette. When his coffee was set before him, in a thick china cup, he spooned in sugar and, stirring, looked up to see that Callie hadn't touched her food.

She said suddenly, 'It isn't true? You're not really selling Crown?'

'When I close the right deal.' Something accusing in her eyes made him add, a little too crisply, 'It's the only sensible thing to do. Crown has hardly been a working ranch at all, these years the Holdens owned it. My father bought it for an investment—Sam Riggs thinks he had ideas of making something out of the place, and finally retiring there; but his plans never worked out. Actually, I think I was the only one ever got any use from the ranch, the times when he used to ship me out here to spend a summer toughening me up.'

'Those hunting trips with Pa.' Callie grinned fondly at the memory. 'With me tagging along like a bird dog. It's a plain wonder you never tanned my britches and sent me home!'

Troy Holden smiled. 'They were good times, weren't they, Callie? But, good times end.'

Her smile faded; her eyes clouded with sympathy. 'I was so sorry,' she exclaimed

22

quickly, 'when I heard about your pa. Wasn't there any warning?'

He shook his head. 'None at all. Later, I learned there'd been an earlier attack that I wasn't told about; and, I didn't know of the troubles with his investments. In fact, I sometimes feel I never really knew my father at all. But I like to think he died the way he would have wanted—in harness.'

'And now, you're to try to pick things up where he dropped them . . .'

'Naturally. Otherwise, everything will go. That's why Crown is so important. Somehow it was overlooked when the estate was liquidated; but the title is clear, and selling it should give me the capital I need to go back into the market and try to salvage at least part of the Holden interests from ruin. If I don't end up broke, that is . . .' Seeing her expression, he smiled and shook his head. 'This is all pretty boring,' he said picking up his coffee cup. 'I couldn't expect it to interest you.'

She watched him as he drank. She said suddenly, 'I'm just wondering if it really interests *you*?'

He looked at her in puzzlement. 'What do you mean?'

'Why, all this talk of big business, and big money—are you sure that's really what you want?'

'It's what I was trained for. It's always been understood I would be taking over for my father, sooner or later. What else would I want?'

'I'm sorry.' She shook her head, self-consciously. 'I had no right to ask. But still, I just can't seem to picture you sitting behind a desk, in one of those big buildings in New York. Not when I've always seen you on a horse, with a rifle in the saddle boot.' She hesitated. 'I—I just can't believe that after Crown is sold we'll none of us be seeing you any more. Ever!'

'Oh, you can't tell about that,' he said. 'I always liked this Montana. I'll probably be back from time to time.'

'Oh, of course!' she retorted. 'Just like your pa did! You'll go and get sucked into that other world and that will be the end of it.'

He smiled, not letting himself be angry with her. 'After all,' he pointed out, turning his cup about in the saucer, 'that *is* my world. Here, I was never really anything but a stranger. My life is back there: my family and friends—the girl I'm going to marry . . .'

The chime of her fork into her plate brought his head up quickly. Her eyes were pinned on him, her cheeks gone suddenly dead white beneath their tan. 'Why, Callie!' he exclaimed, startled and feeling all at once like a clumsy and stupid fool.

'It's all right. I just—' Suddenly her mouth was trembling and she put a hand against it and abruptly turned her head away. He was sure he saw a bright flash of moisture in her eyes. He

24

could only stare at her—stunned by a revelation, and horrified to think of the unintentional hurt he had caused.

It was not intentional that he had never told her of Bea Applegate. The thought had simply never occurred to him, that this girl might imagine she was in love with him!

He was trying to think of something to say, when a shadow fell across the table. Looking up quickly, he saw the pair who stood over them with the smells of horse and of the open night clinging to their clothing. Morgan Peters, looming a head taller than his companion, looked at his daughter's averted face and then swiftly, speculatively, at Holden. Holden saw the danger that narrowed Morgan's eyes and hollowed out his cheeks in a tight-lipped scowl. He said quickly, 'Evening, Morgan.'

There was a resemblance to his brother, the deputy sheriff, but the gaunt face with its beak of a nose was as strong as By Peters' was weak. Gray eyes, beneath a tangled shelf of faded brows, probed at Holden and then, not answering the greeting, the tall man looked again at his daughter.

'Callie? Everything all right here?'

The girl nodded vigorously, but without raising her head. 'Of course, Pa.'

'You sure? I kind of thought, to look at you—'

'I—burnt my tongue on something.'

'Oh.' Peters accepted this, though he still

25

looked doubtingly at the pair seated at the table. Then the scowl smoothed out of his features and his high, broad shoulders appeared to slacken within the flung-open windbreaker he wore. Beside him, Jim Ells—another of the Kettle Creek ranchers, a man of about thirty, with yellow hair that strong Montana suns had bleached out to cornsilk—looked on as though he had missed the undercurrents of feeling here.

Morgan Peters said, 'Holden, Jim and me would like a word with you. We got a proposition to make.' He glanced around the restaurant, which was well filled now with the evening's trade, and busy with talk. 'Kind of noisy here. Maybe we can borrow my brother's office, if you wouldn't mind coming along with us for a few minutes.'

Curious, Troy Holden hesitated as he looked across at the girl. 'Will you excuse us?' She nodded, still avoiding his eyes. He pushed back his coffee cup, and brought out money to leave by his plate in payment for both their orders—though he could see that Morgan Peters didn't too much like this either. Afterward he got his hat off the hook and followed the pair of ranchers, who were already making for the door.

The office at the jail was a tiny cubicle, with barely room in it for a desk and a couple of chairs and a battered filing cabinet. There were two small windows, heavily barred, and a thick

26

slab door opening into a single cell that was almost without light. As they turned in here, Holden and his two companions heard a sudden racket of hoof-sound breaking and growing fast; they halted where they were, to watch a body of a half dozen horsemen come spurring boldly into town.

They brought a tang of lifted dust and lathered horse-flesh and oiled leather as they swept by, with a certain arrogant assurance—looking neither to right nor left, nor easing out of the rolling gait that carried them swiftly on toward the heart of the village. Troy Holden saw the glint of metal on horse trappings and holstered six-shooters and booted rifles. He saw, briefly, the features of the leader who rode straight-up in the stirrups, his head lifted so that the fully risen moon lay plainly across his face. Even that one brief glimpse was enough to hint at the power in the chiseled face, with its massive jaw and full, down-sweeping moustache.

Holden heard a grunt break from Morgan Peters, and as the riders went by and the rush of hoofbeats faded he looked at the rancher. 'Who was that?' he asked, though he already guessed the answer.

'Luke Bartell,' Peters said, and he made the name sound as though it tasted bad.

Young Jim Ells swore bitterly. 'Damned bunch of longriders! Why do they have to pick our town? Why can't they go somewhere else and leave us alone?'

Troy Holden might have said, *Then why don't you try doing something about it?* But he kept silent; and they entered the tiny jail, to find By Peters at the window, peering out into the street where the moon-glimmering sheet of dust was settling in the wake of the vanished riders.

The deputy sheriff turned quickly and the wall lamp touched a faint sheen of sweat on his hollow cheeks. 'Was that who it looked like?'

'It was.' Holden thought Morgan Peters' face held a trace of bitterness as he answered. Surely he knew his brother had been drinking—no doubt there was a half-empty bottle in a drawer of the desk, yonder.

The lawman passed a hand across his cheeks; the hand shook. He seemed to pull himself together with an effort. 'I guess I better get out on the street. A Friday night—a good part of the range in town: I only hope to God nothing happens!'

'It ain't likely,' Morgan assured him. 'Nobody wants trouble with Luke Bartell. But if there's trouble, don't try to manage it single-handed. We're always ready to back you up.'

By Peters nodded, abstractedly. He hitched up his coat, touched the wooden handle of the gun in his holster. He took his hat from a nail behind the door, and drew it on as he walked outside.

28

CHAPTER FOUR

Into the troubled silence, Troy Holden observed, 'From everything I've heard, Bartell and his outfit are rustlers and outlaws. Do they know at the county seat that men like this are riding around the country, just as it pleases them?'

He had asked Sam Riggs the same question and got the same answer. Jim Ells retorted angrily, 'You have any idea how far it is to the county seat? Canada's closer. The law knows Bartell is going to be up and gone across the line before a sheriff's posse can get within hailing distance—it's already happened!'

Morgan Peters broke in, scowling with distaste. 'I'm free to admit Luke Bartell is a thorn in our side,' he admitted gruffly. 'But as long as he lets our herds alone, we at least can live with it. Maybe he'll ride on for other ranges eventually, and leave us in peace.

'Anyway it's a local problem, Holden,' he went on, bluntly changing the subject. 'Not yours. I understand you're fixing to get out from under the ranch your pa left you.'

Holden nodded. 'You heard right.'

'Well, that's why we wanted to see you. What do you say we make ourselves comfortable?' He closed the street door as he indicated the desk and chairs that nearly filled the dingy cubicle. Frankly curious, Troy Holden brought a straight wooden chair away from the wall and took a seat, placing his hat on his knee. Jim Ells hitched himself onto a corner of the desk, a booted leg swinging; he left the only other chair, behind the desk, for Morgan Peters.

The tall man went around and dropped into it, and the ancient barrel chair creaked under his weight; he dropped his dusty, sweated Stetson onto the desktop and leaned to haul open a drawer, saying, 'Ought to be a bottle and glasses here somewhere . . .'

'Don't bother on my account,' Troy Holden said. 'I seldom use it.'

'The hell with it, then.' Peters kneed the drawer shut again. 'Be a sight less trouble in the world if some of us used it less!' Holden wondered, from the bitter tone of his voice, if he wasn't possibly still thinking of his brother.

The rancher leaned his elbows on the desk and laced his fingers together—rope-burned, nicotine-yellowed. He said, 'I'll get right to the point. Jim and I are here on behalf of ourselves, and of the ranches in the valley. We've done a lot of conferring, the past few days, trying to reach an agreement and an offer that we could present to you.'

'An offer for Crown?' At his nod Troy Holden said promptly, 'I'm ready to hear it. It makes no difference to me who I deal with, so long as I get my price.'

Peters and Jim Ells exchanged a look. The

older man cleared his throat uncomfortably. 'You have to understand,' he said gruffly, 'we ain't, any of us, what you'd call rolling in ready cash. The past two winters were tough ones, and the market for beef is still shaky. The point is, even pooling all our credit, we're not in any shape to buy you out.'

In the act of reaching for his cigarettes, Holden paused and frowned in puzzlement from one to the other of the men. 'Then—?'

'What we'd like to try and interest you in is a lease—for as long as you'll give us, on whatever terms we can arrange. Crown has some of the best grass in the valley. Using it for winter range, on shares, the rest of us can start thinking about building up our herds. In the end we may even be in a position where we're able to buy.

'How about it?'

Disappointment made Holden frown. He withdrew his hand, empty, from his pocket. 'Sorry,' he said, more bluntly than he intended. 'A lease is out of the question. I'm selling—now. I thought it was understood.'

'It's understood all right,' Peters said. 'The thing is, we were hoping you might be persuaded to consider a counter offer. But, there isn't any chance of that?'

'No chance at all, I'm afraid.'

Suddenly Jim Ells was off the corner of the desk, standing over him, with a hot fury in his eyes. 'By God,' the blond rancher exclaimed, 'you damn well better consider it! You hear me?'

'Now, Jim!' Morgan Peters exclaimed sharply.

The younger man overrode the protest; anger had been building in him and now it had broken loose, had become a storm of emotion. 'Don't try to shut *me* up. It's him! What does he care about the valley, or anybody in it? It's bad enough that all these years, Crown has had to belong to people like him and his old man— strangers who never set foot on it, from one year's end to another. Now God knows who'll end up owning it. Some syndicate or other, like as not—and us valley people without a word to say in the matter!'

He left off his angry speech, fists clenched and thick chest swelling to his breathing. Troy Holden refused to rise to the baiting; during all this he had remained seated, looking up at the man, only the coldness and stiffness of his face to tell him that he must have lost color under the tongue lashing.

Now Morgan Peters placed both hands upon the desk in front of him, the palms flat. He chose his words with obvious care as he said, into the tense stillness, 'Crown is his, Jim, to do with as he sees fit—and he's not accountable to you, or me, or any of us.' He swung his head to stare at Holden, and his gray eyes—eyes that were very much like his daughter's—were completely cold.

32

'But I regret to say I'm some disappointed in you, mister. Your old man, I couldn't of expected much from. I never saw him again, after that single trip when he had his one and only look at Crown, and bought it. I knew it was nothing but a business matter with him; I can at least say he showed judgment in keeping Sam Riggs on, all these years, to manage the spread for him—since he wasn't interested enough to give it any real attention, himself.

'But you, boy! I got to admit I had a different idea about you. Seeing you from time to time, these past few years, I sort of watched you grow into a man. I sort of thought you had a feel for these mountains—that this high country out here was actually beginning to mean something to you.' He sighed and shrugged. 'But, stands to reason I was bound to be wrong. The way a shoot is shoved into the ground, is the direction it grows.'

It seemed to Troy Holden that, at every turn he took with these people, he found himself in the position of trying to explain and justify himself. It had been that way with Sam Riggs, and with Callie Peters; and now he was growing weary of the attempt. Jim Ells' words still stung; getting to his feet, Holden drew on his hat. 'If we've all had our say, it doesn't appear there's anything more to discuss, does it?'

'There might be one thing,' Peters corrected him, though with a scowling reluctance. 'I'd just as soon not have to bring this up. 'It's my

33

daughter Callie. When Jim and I walked into that restaurant, we could both see that she was crying. She ain't a girl that cries easy; I'm asking you if it was because of something you said or did.'

There was only one answer for that. Stiffly, Troy Holden told him, 'Why don't you ask her? As far as I'm concerned, anything that might have passed between Callie and me was a private matter.' He would have turned and left, with that, but a hand fell on his arm and halted him. He looked around into the face of Jim Ells, thrust belligerently into his own.

Ells was red and his nostrils flared. 'And that's something else you can do—stay the hell away from Callie!' the blond rancher shouted.

It was a cry, and a look, of pure mistaken jealousy. Troy Holden was both surprised and startled, but he felt in no mood just then to indulge the man. 'Not because you tell me,' he retorted sharply, and jerked his arm away.

He wasn't prepared for what happened next. Jim Ells swore and suddenly a hard-knuckled fist was swinging at his face. Holden tried to back away from it. It missed its target, barely grazed his jaw and struck him in the chest with a quick, exploding pain.

His legs tangled with the chair he had quit and he half fell over it, toppling it back against the wall. He twisted about and kept from falling only by colliding full tilt with the wall, catching himself there against both spread

34

hands. As he did so, boots tramped toward him; the overturned chair was kicked out of the way and a hand struck his shoulder and yanked him bodily around.

Ells had his fist cocked and ready, but Troy Holden was not in a mood to take it. Jim Ells was rawhide and sinew, toughened by years of the hardest kind of labor; but Holden, for all his background of money and good living, not only followed the more strenuous forms of hunting but also valued an hour's workout every day in the gym of his New York club. Not knowing this, Ells was open for a surprise. He let Holden slide out from under his hand as he turned, and then a cleanly placed right caught the blond man squarely on one cheekbone.

It was the first time Holden had ever delivered a blow bare-knuckled, without the protection of a padded glove; the pain of it raced shockingly up his arm and exploded. But he saw his assailant's face wiped clean of all expression save that of complete surprise, and Jim Ells was flung backward against the edge of the desk.

Then Morgan Peters was shouting something as he came in between, towering over them both. 'Cut this out!' he cried indignantly. 'Jim, you should be ashamed!' He stared in rebuke at his friend, who was leaning against the desk and fingering his cheek, and panting hard as he glared at Holden in bitter, savage anger. Peters turned to Holden, then, and his face was hard, his voice crisp.

'I'll apologize for what he did,' the big man said. 'But at the same time I'm going to say this, Holden: I ain't the man to let anyone hurt my family. Neither my brother, of whom I ain't too proud—or my daughter that I think more of than life itself. And I got the right, even if Jim hasn't, to ask you to leave Callie alone. From now on, you keep away from her.'

Troy Holden's eyes narrowed slightly. 'Even assuming I had ideas about Callie,' he said crisply, 'don't you think that's taking quite a lot on yourself?'

'All the same,' the rancher said with stern implacability, 'you just see you don't forget it!'

Troy Holden could only stare at these two, outraged by this display of suspicion and—on the part of Jim Ells—of sheer jealousy. His collarbone ached where Ells had struck him, and his knuckles felt sprung and bruised. For his part, he couldn't see that he had done anything at all to apologize for or explain, and a stubborn anger firmed his lips.

He had dropped his hat in the brief scuffle with Ells; he leaned and picked it up, brushed it with a coat sleeve. Holding it, he hesitated a moment; then, not trusting his tongue, he simply turned and walked out, into the moonbright night.

CHAPTER FIVE

He was still trembling a little as he paused to pull on the hat, and straighten the hang of his crumpled jacket. But it was foolish to waste emotion on that scene in the jail office. Peters and Ells should not concern him; soon enough they would no longer even be his neighbors. Meanwhile, the garish spill of light and sound from the Montana House, across the way, was a reminder of a challenge he had been given.

Looking at the lights, and at the line of horses tied out front, he knew he could not afford to let the challenge go—nor was he in a mood to. He filled his lungs with the clean autumn night and let the momentum of his anger carry him deliberately across the street dust, that the moonlight turned to a dull, beaten silver.

As he drew near the saloon, a movement in the shadows near the hitch rack made him pause. At once a voice spoke his name: '*Holden?*'

'Who's there?'

'Ain't anybody—just old Yance Kegley. I been watching out for you.'

The man edged out of the darkness and now Holden could see enough to recognize him— some ancient injury had left the old man with a crippled leg, so that he moved with an odd rolling gait and, when he rode, had to use a shortened stirrup. He made a living of sorts as a wolfer; Holden remembered seeing his shack, during one of his hunting trips in the high hills—he remembered the swaybacked roof and the rotting barn, and the mountainous heap of rusting tins.

He frowned in distaste as he caught the reek of the old man's clothing, that seemed to be imbued with the poisons and chemicals Kegley used in his trade. Holden said stiffly, 'You want something from me?'

The other man might have caught the irritation in his voice. 'From you?' he retorted. 'Not a damn thing! I was about to do you a favor, but I sure as hell don't have to.'

Holden saw he could have made a mistake. There was no point in deliberately antagonizing this disreputable old man; interested now in spite of himself, he said quickly, 'I never turn down a favor. What's on your mind?'

Kegley's ruffled feelings seemed mollified, for after a moment he said in a gruff tone, 'Nothing much—except I been inside there, watchin' Luke Bartell and his boys. Was I you, I'd stay out of there. Bartell's waiting for you, mister!'

'So I understood.'

'And you're goin' in anyway?' Yance Kegley gave a grunt, moved his shoulders inside his worn denim jacket. 'Well, I reckon a man has to choose his own brand of suicide! One thing, though: You might keep your eye on the one dealing solitaire, over at the side table—the Injun, with the snake-skin on his hat. He'll have one hand out of slight. Watch him!'

Troy Holden digested this. He nodded and spoke with real gratitude. 'I thank you for the tip. I promise to keep it in mind.'

He started up the wide steps, and as light from the door struck him more fully he heard the old wolfer's exclamation; 'You ain't even wearing a six-gun!'

'I don't own one,' Holden said. He opened the door and walked inside.

The Montana House was the only saloon in town, and the one place where there were public games. So it did a fair business, though it was anything but fancy—a narrow shoe-box of a room, the long, plain bar facing the banks of felt-topped gaming tables along the opposite side wall. Toward the back were pool tables, a big space-heater sitting in a box of cinders, and an open-front mechanical piano with a bass drum attachment. At the moment, this was not working. When Troy Holden pushed the door shut behind him with his heel, the room was, all of a sudden, deathly quiet. The dry rattle of the bar dice was the last sound to cease.

Perhaps a dozen men were scattered among the card tables; which of them might be Luke Bartell's riders, Holden wasn't in a position to say. Another pair stood alone at the bar—it looked almost as though the regular customers were purposely letting them have it to themselves. For, one of these was the redheaded gunman, Seab Glazer. The dice-thrower turned his head, and again Holden saw the chiseled face, with the bulldog jaw and downsweeping moustache, that he had noticed in the van of the longriders as they swept into town.

Glazer murmured something and Bartell nodded shortly, his black eyes unmoving from Holden as he quietly set down the dice cup.

Cutting his glance sharply to the left, Holden saw—just as Yance Kegley had told him—a man who sat alone with a spread of solitaire laid out on the table in front of him. He had a narrow, hatchet-face, with something of the look of a breed. The crown of his tall black hat was punched out, without creases, the way Indians liked to wear them. And for a hatband he wore the diamond-patterned skin of a bull rattler.

He held the deck of cards in his left hand; sure enough, his right was out of view, somewhere below the table's edge. Eyes as black as obsidian held, unblinking, on the man in the doorway.

If this was the kind Luke Bartell had riding for him, Holden thought, it told all he needed to know of what he was up against.

He refused to give any sign of the alarm bells beating inside him. He walked deliberately forward, placed a hand on the wood and told the man in the apron, 'I'll take Bourbon, friend, if you have it.'

The bartender—actually he was the owner of the Montana House, a black Irishman named Costello, with fists like hams and a single curl of hair plastered to the center of his forehead—was plainly on edge and nervous, as though concerned about his place of business. He gave Holden almost a resentful look, then grudgingly set out a tumbler and filled it from a bottle he took from under the bar. He scooped up the coin Holden put down and, scowling, moved away. Holden drew the shot glass to him but he didn't drink. At that moment the street door opened, drawing his hasty glance. He saw Yance Kegley close the door and sidle, limping, toward a side wall, keeping discreetly out of the way. The old wolfer must have decided he didn't want to miss whatever was to happen . . .

Luke Bartell broke the heavy stillness. 'Your name's Holden?' he said; and, getting a cold stare and a nod: 'Maybe you know who I am?'

'I know.'

'Then we won't have to waste any words.'

He came along the bar, to halt a couple of paces from Holden with Seab Glazer looming at his elbow. Thus confronted, Troy Holden stood his ground. The fingers of his right hand, resting on the bar, turned the half filled whiskey glass and made wet circles on the wood. Bartell said loudly, 'I understand you're stuck with a ranch you're trying to get rid of.'

Holden retorted, 'You should know! I all but

had it sold—before the redhead stepped in.'

Seab Glazer grinned at him wickedly. Bartell merely shrugged. 'Maybe it *was* kind of rough on that rabbit of a man who got run out of town tonight,' the rustler admitted indifferently. 'But it seemed as good a way as any to teach you a few of the facts of life.'

'What facts?'

'Chiefly this one: It don't matter a damn what you *think* you're gonna do with that Crown spread. In the end, you're gonna make your deal with me.'

'With *you*?' Surprise jarred the words out of him, and Holden saw those other eyes narrow and harden.

'That's what I said,' Luke Bartell answered tartly. 'Why—is there something so peculiar in the idea of me owning a piece of cattle range?'

Holden considered the question. 'Some people I've talked to might be inclined to think so.' He shrugged. 'But I suppose what they'd think is neither here nor there.'

'Damned right!' the rustler said, and laid the flat of a hand on the bar. It was a big hand, and powerful, with a saddle of coarse black hair across the back of each rope-scarred finger. 'I've been looking over this country, careful. I've seen a lot of it I like. I like that Crown spread of yours the best of what I seen.

'So name your price, Holden. If it's fair I'll meet it, and no haggling. But, one way or another, I'm taking that spread! What happened tonight should tell you that you'll deal with me, or you won't deal at all!'

Troy Holden felt the weight of every eye, the pressure of every held and lung-trapped breath in that room. Something pulled his glance to a table toward the rear, where a man sat alone with a shot glass and a half-emptied whiskey bottle in front of him. The man lifted his head and Holden saw it was his own foreman, Sam Riggs. After that fruitless quarrel on the hotel veranda, Riggs had stomped away saying he intended to get drunk. From the flushed looseness of his features, it looked as though he was already well on the road—but he was plainly sober enough to understand what was going on in front of him.

The fate of Crown could affect every living being within a radius of miles from this valley, and every man here knew it. Suddenly, as he remembered the pressures he'd been undergoing—not only from Sam but from Morgan Peters and Jim Ells and all the others who resented him, for being different from themselves—Holden thought cynically that it would serve them right, were he to take Bartell's deal and go away and leave them a rustler for a neighbor. In that moment he could almost seem to feel again the weight of Jim Ells' crushing fists . . .

He shook his head. 'I'm afraid not, Bartell,' he said flatly. 'We can't make any deal.'

The big man's head jerked as though in

43

disbelief. A slow flush stained his cheeks. The big hand tightened to a fist. 'And why the hell not?'

'I don't do business with crooks. And I don't take money that almost certainly has blood on it!'

The words were barely out of his mouth when they were drowned in a shout of fury from the redhead, Seab Glazer. He brushed past his chief and came bearing in—one hand reaching for Holden, the other dipping toward the cutaway holster thonged to his leg.

Timing his move, Holden waited until the man was well within range before his hand came off the bar, still holding the glass of Bourbon. He let Glazer have glass and all, squarely in the face; then, as the redhead yelled and doubled up, pawing at his streaming eyes, stepped forward to seize hold of the gunman and, half turning him, propel him across the narrow width of the room. The one with the snakeskin hatband was starting—belatedly—to bring up the six-shooter he had been holding in his lap. Glazer struck the table and upended it, slamming it into the seated man, and they both went down in a tangle of smashed wood and a spray of spilled playing cards.

The gun popped out of the breed's fingers, hit the floor spinning and came sliding across the boards, straight toward Holden, who had been meaning to dive for cover around the street-end of the bar. Now, instead, he leaned

44

and scooped the gun off the floor and came up with it leveled and ready.

'I'll use this,' he said tersely, 'if I have to!'

Bartell must have thought he meant it, for the big rustler froze where he stood—his right hand just brushing back the skirt of his coat, to clear the holster strapped beneath. The ones Holden had floored came rolling free of the table's wreckage now, Glazer swearing furiously and pawing still at his streaming eyes; they too caught sight of the weapon in Holden's grasp. As they went motionless he straightened, hoping no one could see the violent shaking of his knees or the sweat he felt upon his face.

Keeping his voice firm he told Bartell, 'I might as well make it clear: I'm a stubborn man. I meant what I said about no deal—and you won't change my mind, by sending toughs like the redhead at me!'

Bartell's blocky face was a mixture of dangerous emotions. About to speak, he turned his head sharply: Holden saw reflected, in the bar mirror, what it was had drawn his attention—the wolfer, leaning forward where he stood against the wall and showing all his teeth in a grin of wicked delight.

You might have thought this scene was being played strictly for Yance Kegley's benefit and his amusement. But when he saw Bartell's savage stare turned on him, the grin died and the old man hastily drew back, obviously not so happy about being noticed. Luke Bartell dismissed him, then, turning back to the man who had dared to challenge him, 'Holden, you may be tougher than I thought,' he said grudgingly. 'I won't make that mistake again. But, tough or not, you're a fool if you think you can pull a bluff on me!'

Anger began to have its way with Troy Holden, swamping the voice of caution. 'How would you like to go to the devil?' he snapped. 'Just stay away from me. Stay away from Crown. And after this, leave my buyers alone!'

Pure ugliness peered at him from Luke Bartell's eyes. The mouth behind the heavy moustache pulled down into a snarl. 'Why, you damned dude! I'll tell you what's going to happen: There won't be no buyer. I'll take that ranch away from you—on my own terms!' Suddenly, to a flip of his thumb, a blur of gold streaked toward Holden. By reflex Holden plunked the coin out of the air, left-handed, and looked at what he held in his palm.

A gold eagle. Twenty dollars.

'There's my terms,' Bartell said. 'You'd best put it in your pocket; because after what just happened it's every cent you're going to get! It don't matter whether you take it or not—I'm going to run your tail clean out of this country!'

Troy Holden raised his cold stare to the outlaw's face. He looked at Seab Glazer and the breed, who had climbed to their feet and stood hating him with their eyes. He looked around at the other silent faces that filled the room with a tension that was almost like the throbbing of a pulsebeat.

Without a word he flung the coin, ringing, in front of Bartell's scuffed boots. And laying the six-gun on the bar he turned and left the Montana House. His movements were deliberate and unhurried, but the sudden cold blast that struck his body, as the glass door swung beneath his shaking hand, told him nearly every inch of him was drenched with sweat.

CHAPTER SIX

At the livery barn Troy Holden found the old hostler dozing, shook him awake and told him to fetch his horse. Waiting, he stood and looked at the village and listened to the quiet sounds of the night, while he forced his nerves to unwind.

No one came near him; there was no immediate hint of a sequel to that encounter at the Montana House. Later, he was checking the cinch and preparing to put toe in stirrup when someone came stumbling toward him up the hoof-splintered ramp. He turned quickly, and saw it was Sam Riggs.

The foreman showed the whiskey he'd been drinking. In the yellow light of a lantern on a roof prop, his face looked swollen and he swayed a little. 'Here you are, Holden!' he grunted. 'I been huntin' all over. Tried the hotel, but they hadn't seen you . . .'

'I'm riding back to Crown! I'm too keyed up for bed.' Making no comment on Riggs' obvious condition, he added, 'What happened in the bar? After I left?'

Riggs gave a low whistle. 'That was a scene! Glazer, and that breed they call Wasco—after what you done to 'em, they really wanted blood; but Bartell shut 'em up. He said—' The foreman hesitated, then blurted it out: 'He said you was nothing but blow. He said you're still just a damned dude, and he's giving odds you'll be out of the country by morning!'

Holden's tight smile was icy. 'Has he had many takers?'

'Look, Mr. Holden!' Urgent feeling drew Riggs an anxious step nearer, and he lurched giddily and put a hand against a roof timber to steady himself. 'What you done in there tonight—that sure wasn't blow, and it wasn't bluff! I'll say it made a liar out of *me*! I think of the things I said this evening—and the things I thought and didn't say . . .'

'Don't bother,' Holden said, cutting across his apology. 'I made a stupid play to the grandstands, that could have got me killed— and it accomplished nothing.'

'The point is, you stood up to Luke Bartell! I don't know another man that ever tried it!

Least of all, a—a—' He fumbled for words.

'A damned dude?' Troy Holden supplied. 'Let me tell you something, Sam. Where I come from, I've known crooks who make Bartell look like nothing! They're twice as tough in their own way and they're every bit as dangerous—even if they do sit behind mahogany desks, in padded chairs, and wouldn't know one end of a six-gun from the other. The Holdens have never knuckled under to men like that, and I'm not going to start with a cowcountry tough like Bartell.'

'All the same,' Riggs insisted, 'you better watch your step with him.' He added, dropping the subject, 'If you're riding, give me time to get my horse and I'll go along.'

Holden looked at him, smelling the whiskey on him, and shook his head. 'I'm afraid I'd have to hold you in the saddle. No—you stay in town and sleep it off. Besides, I have something I want you to do for me tomorrow: Wait till the stage gets back from the railroad and if there's any mail, bring it out to the ranch.'

Riggs looked at him shrewdly, and Holden knew the foreman understood he was still preoccupied with the letter which hadn't been waiting at the stage line office. Sam Riggs nodded and then said, as he remembered, 'There was something too, about some telegrams you wanted sent . . .'

Troy Holden shook his head. 'They'll have to wait. I can't sell anyone a pig in a poke. Until this threat from Bartell is cleared up—one way or another—any buyer I brought in to look at Crown could be put through the same thing that happened to George Lunceford tonight. I can't allow that, not again!'

'Then I reckon we've got a job ahead of us!'

Troy Holden only nodded moodily, and swung into the saddle. Some of his own restiveness of spirit seemed to convey itself to the horse and he had to use the bit to curb it down as it swung about, shod hooves trampling the splintered floorboards. After that, Holden rode out through the wide doors, ducking his head for clearance, and down the ramp to the street. He scarcely heard Sam Riggs' anxious parting words: 'If it was me, I'd keep my eyes open!'

He swung the bay into the intersection of the cross street, full into the silver wash of moonlight, and would have sent it directly on toward the junction with the north valley trail; but he saw movement on the porch of the hotel and heard Callie Peters call his name across the dust. As he reined over that way, she came out from under the roof overhang, onto the steps. Their faces were almost on a level as Holden pulled in, without dismounting.

She was breathless with concern. 'Troy! What are you trying to do to yourself? Walking into that place, that way—alone! Challenging Luke Bartell and his whole outfit!'

Irritably he demanded, 'How did you know?'

'Why, Sam Riggs told us—just now, when he was here looking for you. I almost died!'

'It wasn't as bad as all that. And nothing came of it.'

She insisted, 'But it could! They'll never let it end there! Don't you see?' Her words broke in a sound that was almost like a sob. Then, before Holden could think of any answer, they were interrupted. Big Morgan Peters emerged from the shadows of the veranda; he shaped up tall and lean against the lobby lights as he came out to stand beside his daughter.

The rancher said sharply, 'Girl, ain't you being just a little silly about this?' His head swung, and Holden could almost feel the eyes boring at him from below the brim of the man's hat. 'I have to admit, you got more guts than I pegged you for, Holden—even if I can't say as much for your common sense, taking the kind of chances you do!' Grudging as it was, Holden knew that was the nearest to a compliment he was going to get from the man; and it was immediately tempered by an ill-natured reminder: 'All the same, I hope I don't have to repeat what I told you before.'

What he meant was, his warning about staying away from Callie. Just now he wasn't even making allowance for the fact that this scene was his daughter's doing, calling Troy Holden across the street to speak to him. Stiffly Holden said, 'I remember, all right. Maybe *you'll* remember what I answered!' Turning to

51

the girl, then, he touched a finger to hatbrim and said, a trifle stiffly, 'Good night, Callie. And don't worry—nothing will happen to me. You'll be seeing me again.'

On that note he sent the bay ahead. He could imagine Callie's bewilderment over the cryptic exchange—and likely as not, her father's smoldering anger. And now a quick spurt of flame drew his glance to someone he hadn't noticed before, on the walk below the veranda's splintered railing. The match was carried to the bowl of a pipe; its glow revealed the face of the yellow-haired rancher, Jim Ells. His stare met Holden's above the flame as, deliberately, he sucked fire into the bowl of the pipe, his cheeks drawing in.

And Troy Holden rode on, feeling the eyes of the two men and the girl on him as he went ahead up the crooked street—wondering too, uneasily, just how many others watched him go.

That same uneasiness traveled with him, even when he had put the town at his back and there was only the night with its sharp contrasts of black and silver, and the shouldering masses of rock and pine ridges. He had been more tense than he realized—the encounter with Bartell had tapped reserves of energy, and coming on top of his other frustrations of the night it left him edgy and ill-tempered. He had never thought of this country as containing personal enemies—men who might even like to see him dead. It was a new concept and an unpleasant one, that put nagging worry at the back of his mind to grow stronger as the minutes passed.

He began to feel his aloneness and his vulnerability, so much so that an odd prickling made itself uncomfortably present along his spine. Somehow he had a sense of other riders abroad in the night. A wind had come up, raising a sound of surf in the pine tops; but once he was so certain he had heard hoofbeats striking bare rock, somewhere on the trail behind him, that taut nerves jerked the rein and made the bay horse halt and stomp in protest. Troy Holden cursed the rattle of bit chains, that interfered with his hearing. Settling the bay, he pulled into the dense shadow of a thicket while he searched the murmuring wind that blew up from the south.

Nothing—no further sound; and though he waited a good ten minutes, no horseman appeared. Nerves and imagination, he told himself. But even as he did he could think of other explanations.

If that was another horseman, following him from town, he could have guessed he'd let himself be heard; he could be waiting now for Holden to decide he was mistaken, and start on again. Or, if you assumed he knew this hill country—and whoever he was, it stood to reason he must know it better than Troy Holden—then there was no real reason for him to keep to the trail at all. The wagon trace followed the easiest grades, snaking down from that bottleneck pass where the stage road linked Kettle Creek with the outside world; on a night of such clear moonlight, a rider could easily pick a more direct route.

As his horse grew tired of standing still and turned restless under him, Holden became angry at the futile waste of time and finally put the bay into the trail again. And, riding on, he found his uneasiness giving way to other feelings.

All those people tonight—Sam Riggs and Luke Bartell and Seab Glazer; Jim Ells and Morgan Peters and the latter's drunken brother. Yes, and even Callie! He resented the way every single one of them seemed bent on involving him in matters that held no personal interest for him. He had tried to explain to Callie that this was not his world. It had no claims on him—it could do no more than delay him from getting back to those other people and affairs that were his prime concern. He shook his head, as a baffled impatience arose in him and closed off his senses to the beauty of the night—to the ridges like black cutouts, the wide sky and the milky disc of the moon whose glow blanked out the near stars . . .

The land leveled off finally; this twisted wagon road shook free of its kinks and became a straight pencil-line that cut directly down through dense jackpine. Below, the valley lay like a half inflated sack, pointing northward within its sheltering fold of ridges. Where the trail took its final turn, a boulder the size of a small house crowded the timber. When he rounded this a nighthawk whisked by in silent but sudden flight, so close to him that he ducked involuntarily.

The bay swung its head; thinking it was the bird that had startled it, Holden spoke and tightened the reins. A bare instant later, he realized his mistake when another horse snorted, somewhere to his immediate left.

His head whipped about sharply, even as he felt the bay's barrel swell to an answering whicker. Against the shadow of the big rock he glimpsed a dark shadow that could only be a horse with a rider motionless on its back. His hand pulled the rein involuntarily just as a gun spoke, in a smash of sound and a smear of muzzleflame.

He felt the bullet spear into him. If the horse hadn't been moving away he likely would have been swept from the saddle. Instead, lurching wildly, he managed to catch at the horn. He heard his own voice yelling at the animal, and somewhere found the strength and presence of mind to drum both heels into its flanks.

The bay gave a squeal and lunged straight ahead, down that alley of moonlight descending through the trees. As it did so, either the same gun or another spoke again—behind them now, its roar battering against the face of the big rock. The blow struck solidly. It lifted Holden, slammed him forward onto the neck of his horse.

After that he knew he must be falling, but it felt rather as though he went spinning away into some black and engulfing nowhere.

CHAPTER SEVEN

He was conscious of pain that was too general to be localized, and an odd and unnatural sensation of motion. It came to him that his head and limbs were without support, and that they were dangling and swaying in a way that vaguely alarmed him and, as it continued, filled him with nausea.

Dull agony blocked his thought processes, but he became enough aware to realize he lay jackknifed across a creaking saddle, bound there, and rocking helplessly as the horse under him picked a way over uneven and tough terrain. When he opened his eyes he could see nothing but the vaguest blur of dark ground sliding beneath him. He tried to cry out in protest and lift his head, and immediately regretted the effort it cost.

But abruptly the movement ceased, though he felt the jar as the animal beneath him stomped restlessly a time or two. Another horse moved up beside him, a voice he thought he should recognize spoke somewhere harshly:

56

'Hell's fire! Will you take it easy? I'm doing the best I can!'

Holden tried to mutter something in answer, but he was already sliding again into the muffling recesses of unconsciousness.

*   *   *

... He was still lying face down, but the torturing motion had ceased. Unable to move, he had his face pressed against some fetid-smelling material that might be dirty bedclothes; he could breathe only poorly and it was likely some deep-buried fear of suffocation that roused him. When he opened the one eye that he could see with, it was to stare directly into a blazing yellow flame set only inches away. He blinked and groaned.

The light was a kerosene lamp, on a box or table beside his bed. Now a hand moved it away, and the same voice he had heard before spoke gruffly: 'You pick a poor time to come around, mister! You may not know it, but you got a rifle slug in your back—pressing right against your spine. I'm just now fixing to get it out of there.'

Holden saw a glint of reflected light, glancing from metal. It looked like the blade of a butcher knife. Horror roused him, actually lifting his head a trifle out of the musty blankets. 'Not with that, damn you!' he tried to say, hearing only a croaking protest from his

57

own lips. Then a bent knee came down, hard, upon his naked shoulders and pressed him flat again, and the voice said, 'You're gonna hold still, you hear—if I have to set on your head to make you do it!'

There was no strength in him to struggle. He lay like that, pinned and helpless—and then the blade bit home, and Troy Holden learned to the core of his being what pain really was. He shouted, his whole body arching like a taut bow. After that, mercifully, all consciousness drained from him.

How much later he could not know, he lay unmoving and awake, all strength seemingly spent beyond recovery. There was no desire in him to move; he scarcely comprehended how long he had been aware of himself, and of the world to which he'd returned. Remembering, then, what had gone before, he sent down tentative probes of awareness—until they met a deep center of dull, throbbing ache somewhere toward the middle of his back. Hastily he withdrew them.

He must have let out a groan. Someone moved into his field of vision and this time he recognized Yance Kegley. The old wolfer said sharply, 'You better take it easy, there!'

Holden's throat felt swollen, unapt for speech. When he tried to shift his head a little the muscles at the back of his neck protested. At the second effort he brought out something that sounded like, 'Where am I?'

The cripple made it out, apparently. 'My shack—where else?' he answered. 'And in my own damn bunk!'

'How long?'

'Well, this is Sunday afternoon. In case you don't remember, it was Friday evening somebody boosted you out of the saddle with a couple of thirty-caliber slugs!'

Troy Holden groaned again. He closed his eyes again for a moment, fighting the draining lethargy and listening to the old man move about the room in his warped, crippled way. After a moment he was able to ask, 'Did you manage to carve the bullet out of me? You and that butcher knife?'

At that Kegley chuckled, obviously pleased with himself. 'Like prying the pit out of a cherry. Damned thing near popped up and hit me in the eye. Want a look?'

He dug in a pocket, held out a horny palm containing a battered chunk of lead. Holden focused his eye on the bullet, and grimaced. 'Keep it for a souvenir!'

'I ain't no sawbones,' the old man said blandly. 'Still, I think I done a pretty good job, considering. Didn't have to carve you up too bad, and the hole looks clean enough. But the slug was lyin' right against your spine. Reckon the test will be when we find out if you got any life in your legs, at all.'

'You may have to wait a while for that,' Holden said grimly.

He felt sickened at the thought of the crude butchery that had been done on him, and at the moment felt a dread of testing the results. The drained weakness settled on him again, and the world splintered and melted once more into darkness.

After that came an undetermined succession of waking and unconsciousness, that went on for he knew not how long. Once, during one of his clear moments, Troy Holden asked, 'Do you have any idea who it was that ambushed me?'

There was the slightest pause before the old man answered, and Holden was to wonder afterward if perhaps he was lying when he said finally, 'I never seen nobody. I was riding home and I heard the shots, not too far ahead. When I got to you, you were lying in the trail and I could hear a horseman going through the timber—like maybe I'd scared him off, coming along like that.'

'It was no more than one rider? You're positive of that?'

'I listened for a long time, to make sure. Then I looked you over—thought you was dead, at first, but soon seen you wasn't. So I caught up your horse and got you across the saddle and headed for here.'

'And I'm eternally grateful to you,' Troy Holden said carefully. 'Only—I'm wondering why you couldn't have taken me back to town instead.'

'Because I wasn't goin' that direction,'

Kegley retorted, as though it were the most reasonable explanation in the world; and for the first time it occurred to Holden, with a faint thrill of dread, that he might be in the hands of a madman. 'Besides,' the old man went on, 'there ain't no real sawbones hereabouts—not anybody who could of done a better job than I did. I figure, at the very best, you're gonna be laid up and pretty near helpless for quite some time to come.

'Supposing whoever wanted to murder you found he hadn't quite managed. If you was in town, or somewhere handy—what would keep him from making a second try? And what could you do but lie there and let him?'

That hadn't occurred to Holden, and it made a horrible kind of sense. But at once it suggested something else: 'How do you know he won't find our tracks, and follow us both here?'

'He won't follow no tracks,' Yance Kegley said flatly. 'Don't think I'm such a fool I left any for him! That's a much traveled road. Whoever notched you ain't gonna have any luck reading sign on it. Especially after I brushed out the evidence where you fell off your horse. He may not even know for sure he got a hit.

'No—take it from me: For the time being at least, you're safe enough . . .'

Troy Holden let himself breathe more easily. Crazy the old man might be, but plainly there was a lot of cunning craftiness to him too.

Probably he'd made the whole grisly business into a game, taking a half-demented delight in out-witting the would-be assassin.

As though satisfied, some deep-seated instinct for self-preservation seemed to let go. He sank again into oblivion, but deeper than before into a nothingness that was broken only by rare moments of lucidity. Somehow he was aware that Yance Kegley was taking care of his needs—changing the dressings on his wounds, even managing now and then somehow to get food inside him. His mind was willing to have it so, while his body went about its essential work of mending the hurts that had nearly done for him.

Time, as such, meant nothing. But there came a moment when he surfaced, and realized he was more fully aware than on any such previous occasion—and, for the first time, interested in his surroundings.

He still felt more or less dead from the waist down, but he didn't let himself think of that just yet. He lay on his back, a pillow under his head, a blanket drawn over him. Above him were rafters, laid with a crude ceiling of rough-adzed timbers. In one corner, cleats nailed to a pole made a ladder, rising to a square hole and a trapdoor to the loft.

Turning his head, he had a view of a crude-looking cabin that seemed to contain no more than a single room. Whatever it was let in the daylight, he judged it was not glass but more likely some kind of oiled skin. It showed him walls of chinked logs, furniture put together from split poles and rawhide—a couple of graceless straight chairs, a rickety-looking table. A fire burned in a mud and brick fireplace, with shelves nearby holding food and supplies. Odds and ends of clothing hung from pegs, and a rifle hung above the door. In one corner, partially hidden by the table, he saw a disorderly heap of what looked to be traps of various sizes.

The smell of the room was compounded pungently of grease and stale food and tobacco and dirty clothes, and something else that could be the stink of a wolfer's baits and poisons.

Suddenly the door opened—dragging the floor, on poorly hung leather hinges—and Yance Kegley entered. Looking past him Troy Holden saw, in some astonishment, a blank whiteness and a swirl of snow that followed the old man in on a blast of icy air. He had an armload of chopped wood balanced in the crook of an elbow. He worried the door shut, limped over to the fireplace and dropped his load beside it. Afterward, turning away, the old man ripped open the fastenings of his heavy coat.

The coldness he had brought in seemed to cling to him and his clothing. He took a briar pipe, had it halfway to his lips when he saw Holden looking at him.

The pipe halted in mid-air. Kegley grunted and stared at the injured man, across its unlighted bowl. 'So! You decided to join the living.'

'I'll let you know!' Troy Holden answered gruffly. He was eyeing with growing concern the snow that clung wetly to the old man's clothing. Suspiciously he demanded, 'Just what day is this?'

Kegley cocked an eyebrow at him. 'Why, it's the twenty-fourth of November. Yesterday was Thanksgiving.'

'Good God! Don't tell me I've lain in this bed for five weeks!'

'Well, I'll say you ain't been doing much traveling,' Kegley agreed dryly. He frowned at the hurt man. 'You mean to say that you wasn't even conscious, all that time? Why, hell! You've been awake, off and on. You've talked to me.'

'I must have been out of my head. But I don't think I am now.'

'You do seem on the mend.' The old man pulled off his coat and hat, shook the snow from them and hung them up. He shoved some more wood onto the fire, and turned back to his patient. 'Still a ways to go, though,' he said. 'Hole in your chest ain't making any real trouble—bullet missed touching the lung, and didn't damage the ribs too much. But it's that other one . . .' He flipped back the blanket, uncovering Holden's lower legs. He pointed a

64

gnarled finger. 'See them things down there? Them's your feet. Mister, you still got me all-fired curious to know if you can move them any. Suppose you show me!'

Holden looked down the length of his body. Suddenly, despite the chill of the room a faint sweat broke out upon his cheeks. He heard himself begin to stammer: 'I—I don't—'

'Damn you!' Yance Kegley looked all at once twice his actual height, standing over the crude bunk and glaring at him in scathing anger. 'You ain't even trying! I pegged you for having more gumption than this. Could be I was wrong?'

Staring back at his tormentor, Holden felt something akin to active hatred. He still had that horrible nothingness, there at the middle of his spine, and when he tried to focus his attention there he became aware of a core of pain that made him rebel against testing himself against it. But there was no escaping the cruel contempt of Yance Kegley's hypnotic stare; under its prodding, Troy Holden set his jaw and his hands drew up into fists and he watched his feet—curious objects, that seemed no part of him at all—move a few wavering inches away from each other and settle back again.

At once, old Kegley was grinning as though the triumph had been his own. 'That's more like it—makes one thing, at least, you don't have to worry about any more.' He rubbed hard palms together, with a faintly rasping sound.

'Now, then, how about some grub?'

'Since you mention it,' Troy Holden admitted, 'I don't feel as though I'd ever eaten.'

'Another good sign,' the old man said, nodding. 'I'll put something together.' He turned to it.

Holden was suddenly weak with relief; he hadn't realized how deeply anxious he was, at the root of his being, over the effects of that bullet Kegley had dug out of him. Lying there, watching the old wolfer set about the chore of preparing a meal, he said suddenly, 'I realize I'll never be able to repay what I owe you.'

He expected Kegley to agree, with more of his acid sarcasm; instead, the old man merely looked at him most oddly. When he spoke it was to say, 'I'm surprised you ain't asked me any questions about the state of your affairs, down the valley . . .'

Thought of the people of Kettle River had frankly not occurred to him; it was more or less with indifference that he asked, 'They know yet who it was shot me?'

'They don't even know you been shot!'

Kegley carried a smoke-blackened coffeepot to the door, stepped out long enough to scoop snow into it and returned to hang it over the fire. He saw the look of astonishment on Holden's face, then, and he said with some heat, 'Did you think I'd let the news out—warn your enemies, so they could come up here while you were lying helpless and finish you

66

off? And do for me at the same time, like as not?'

Holden saw the sense of this argument, but he could only shake his head. 'In the Lord's name, then—what *do* people think happened to me?'

'Well, now, I reckon they think you pulled out.' Kegley was turning the handle of a coffee mill, seemingly unaware of the enormity of what he was saying. 'That night in the Montana House—when you stood up to Luke Bartell— he warned you not to try and stay around this country. From what I've heard folks sayin' they've all about decided you must have thought things over, and decided to do like he told you.'

'They think I turned tail and ran from him?' Troy Holden groaned, aghast at the thought. He added bitterly, 'That must make Bartell feel pretty pleased with himself!'

'I reckon.' Kegley dumped the contents of the mill into the coffeepot. 'You see, there's a trifle more I got to tell you. Luke's taken over your ranch.' He nodded, to the look on Holden's face. 'Yep. Something like a week after you disappeared. Him and his boys just rode into Crown, told Sam Riggs and the rest of your crew to go lose themselves, and took charge.'

Holden stammered: 'That's fantastic! They couldn't have!'

'Who was to stop 'em—those neighbors of

yours? Morg Peters, and Jim Ells, and so on? By the time they even heard about it, the thing was done. Hell! Bartell knew he was too tough for the whole bunch of them, put together!'

'But—' He started to say, *the law*! But then he thought of By Peters and knew the answer to his question—knew he had been all over that ground before, the night he argued with Sam on the steps of the hotel in Reserve.

Kegley had guessed his thought. 'Even supposing the sheriff's man around here amounted to a damn,' he pointed out, 'without you who's there even to prefer charges? Luke Bartell said he'd have Crown, and it looks like he figures he can bluff it out and keep his word. And so far it looks like he's doing it!'

If there was any doubt remaining that Luke Bartell's had been the scheming mind, and the will, behind the bullets that knocked Troy Holden from the saddle that night, they were gone now. But Troy Holden said grimly, 'Luke Bartell could be in for a surprise!'

'Not for a while, anyway,' the old wolfer reminded him dryly, and went to fetch a mixing bowl and a sack of flour off the shelf. 'With holes like them there in you, I see another couple or three months before you'll even be getting around with a cane. I been in about the same place you are now, boy,' he added, slapping his gimp leg, crippled in an ancient injury. 'I reckon I should know how long it takes. Meanwhile, I hope you'll remember: If

Bartell *should* get wind that you're still alive, and find out where you are—it could go real bad for the both of us!'

Holden, thinking this over, saw the truth of it. But it helped not at all to fight the sudden rush of bitter impatience that surged through him and left him helpless and shaken. He lay a moment, digesting what he'd learned, scowling as he watched the old man at his work.

He said suddenly, 'I want to write a letter. Independent of what happens to Crown, there are people, back East where I came from, that have been waiting too long to hear from me. Business that no one else can handle . . .'

'Why, that's all right with me,' Kegley said, with a lift of his shoulders. 'Sure, you can write—all the letters you hanker to. Only, don't expect to get 'em mailed, right soon.'

'Why not?'

For answer, Yance Kegley jerked his head toward the plank door. A gust of wind, hitting the shack just then, shook its walls with staggering force. 'Hell! You seen what it's like out there. This storm started day before yesterday. Rate it's building, I ain't expecting to make it into town inside a couple weeks at the least—and by then the stage roads will likely be closed for the winter.

'Still, don't let me stop you if you got the itch to do some writing. I think there's paper and pencil somewhere.'

He started peering aimlessly about for them.

Troy Holden sank back upon the musty pillow, defeated. 'Don't bother!' he muttered, and saw the old man's face break into a cruelly mocking grin.

CHAPTER EIGHT

In his several visits to this country Troy Holden had heard tales of Montana winters, but he had never thought to experience one himself. Now, in Yance Kegley's shack in the hills above Kettle Creek range, he found himself caught up in something Kegley assured him would go down in the book.

Days on end the snow descended from a blank, swollen sky; angry winds buffeted the cabin and the pines on the white-shrouded slopes were lost in a blind smother. Kegley tied ropes from his door to barn and woodshed, so that he could manage his chores and find his way back, snow-encrusted and half-frozen, to the safety of his roof and his fireplace. And the weeks dragged on.

Of much of this, Holden was scarcely conscious. He existed in a region of pain and mending tissues, and such thoughts as he had were for that other world, a couple of thousand miles away from this storm-locked cabin, where even now his fate was being decided. He had no illusions. High finance waited on no man. The months he lay helpless here were a critical time of battles which, through his absence, he was losing by default.

It was when he thought of Bea Applegate that he ground his teeth in pure frustrated agony.

His wounds were healing—a slow process, but after all he had nothing else to do but wait it out. A day came when he ventured to try his legs, with Yance Kegley's help. Out of bed, he tottered from weakness and nearly fell; but he rallied his courage and his strength and even managed a step or two, and knew then that he was whole again. He practiced daily, hobbling about the cabin at first like an old man until wasted muscles began to regain their strength.

He had heard the old-timers speak of something called 'cabin fever,' and now he learned what they meant: Two men, shut up like this in a space small enough that either one, alone, might have wearied of the confinement, began to find each other's company a graveling burden. There came moments, during that long winter, when Holden really began to wonder about his companion's sanity, and to cast about for means to protect himself if the old man grew violent.

Kegley would yell at him, cursing him for taking up his bed and eating his grub and not lifting a hand to the chores. At first Holden promised that he would be paid, and paid well,

71

for his inconvenience; eventually he merely clamped his jaws and tried to shut his ears, and refused to answer. He owed the old man his life, and he knew it. But there were times when he caught the fever, himself—when he seemed to feel the walls closing in on him and when old Kegley's ugly face, and his movements as he limped grotesquely about the dismal shack, seemed completely hateful.

He took refuge in reading. Kegley owned two books—an outdated almanac, and a dog-eared volume with its front cover ripped away which turned out to be an ancient copy of Scott's *Ivanhoe*. Holden had never been much of a reader but he went through both these volumes twice, escaping into them when he thought he would go mad if he lay any longer doing nothing. The old man, meanwhile, hunched at the table and engrossed himself in unending games of solitaire with a pack of greasy cards, wetting one splayed thumb each time he dealt a card.

One night Holden awoke and lay in the darkness, listening to an unfamiliar sound. It took him a moment to place it. There was the wind, pummeling the mud-chinked walls; but there was something else: water, dripping from the eaves. Melt water! He almost shouted to rouse Kegley where the old man lay wrapped in furs and blankets on the bare floor; then thought better of it. Let the old man sleep! He lay listening to the cheerful sound outside, not daring to believe, until it lulled him to sleep again.

'Chinook!' old Kegley told him next morning, his toothless mouth grinning. 'Listen to her blow! That south wind can eat up the snow so quick that you can see the drifts shrink!' But then native cruelty made him add, grinning, 'Only, don't get your hopes too high. Could be another blizzard blow in from Canada by tomorrow. Even if it don't, the stage roads ain't gonna be open for another month or better.

'So, lay back and relax. You ain't going nowhere soon!'

The wind changed. More snow fell. But at last it became evident the back of the winter was broken. The big blizzards never returned; the chinook kept blowing, and the drifts shrank in runnels flashing under the warming sun, and black earth began to appear. One day Kegley saddled up and rode out on his rawboned sorrel horse, his rifle across his knees. He came back toting the tongue and haunches cut from a buck deer—almost the first fresh meat since winter closed its iron grip on them.

Now real restlessness seized hold of Troy Holden, and set him prowling. Wearing a windbreaker the old man lent him, he went out to try his legs in the clearing where Kegley's shack stood. The feel of sun and fresh air, and solid earth under his feet, revived him wonderfully. He walked further every day; he saddled the bay for short rides into the thawing hills. He even tried his hand with the ax, splitting firewood and stacking it in the woodshed, which was itself a storehouse for all the strange agglomeration of junk the old man had scrounged in his wanderings through the hills—Holden even saw a box of dynamite sticks, the box stenciled with the name of the mining operation from which Kegley had probably stolen it.

There was agony at first, and then exhilaration, in stretching mended muscles and feeling them respond to the demands he put on them. But his return to health, and the easing of winter on this Montana high country, brought him face to face with his problem. The key to it was starkly simple: The key was Crown. It was still the only asset left him—and it was in the hands of Luke Bartell. Somehow, he must contrive to get it back—and while he was at it, he promised himself with bleak definiteness, he would repay someone for the agony of a bullet in the back, and for the terror of wondering if he would ever walk again.

He had a reckoning due him—overdue. If his enemies had thought him a dude who would break and run at the first real threat, they might learn what months of suffering could do to temper and harden a man into someone they could not ignore.

One thing—he had been taught patience. He would husband his strength, wait till he was fully ready before he made his move. Even after the breaking weather made it possible for him to leave Kegley's, he continued to bide his time. On his rides in the hills he took along Yance Kegley's six-shooter—an ancient Smith & Wesson, converted to cartridges—and a box of shells he bought from the old man. He spent time practicing with the gun, shooting at marks, learning something about a hand-gun. He had always been good with a rifle; he had a feeling that skill with a six-shooter was something he might soon find valuable.

As he rode back to the cabin at the tail end of such a day, with melt water flashing and runneling from under snow-banks, he felt that he was very nearly ready. There was still a dull center of throbbing ache low in his back, that especially bothered him when he was tired; he hoped that would go away in time. Whatever his program for striking back at his enemies, he might as well get on with it. For one thing, he'd long since worn out his welcome at Kegley's. Old Yance, he was sure, would be more than glad to see the last of him . . .

He rode out of the mouth of a rocky draw and pulled in abruptly.

The sprawl of cabin and outbuildings lay just below him, beyond a belt of timber. The door of the horse shed stood open; Kegley was cleaning out the place, using shovel and wheelbarrow and beating a path across the muddy slop of the yard to a manure pile below the corral. What had caught Holden's attention was a pair of riders who were making their way across a boulder-strewn stretch of mountain meadow, coming toward the shack at such an angle that so far, at least, they seemed to have escaped the notice of the old man working around the horse shed.

Holden frowned, considering. He could not see those riders clearly, at this distance, but there was something about one of them that reminded him sharply of one of Luke Bartell's men. The breed they called Wasco . . .

He spoke to the horse and sent it down the slope, keeping to such cover as he could as he dropped toward the band of pine and new-leafed aspen. He lost the riders, and the buildings. He was wearing an old windbreaker Kegley had lent him, and as he rode he dug into a pocket and drew out the Smith & Wesson. Moments later, breaking through the trees, with the blind side of the shack just before him, he heard a pair of horses arriving in the muddy yard beyond.

Holden dismounted, looked about for a place to tie the reins and finally made hasty anchor to a bush that had sprung up close to the wall of the house. Gun ready, he went at a quick prowl to a forward corner where he hoped he could see what was going on.

The horsemen were just pulling rein, their animals stepping around under them in the slop and the rotten, melting rags of snowdrifts.

One of them was Wasco, sure enough—Holden recognized the steeple-crowned hat with the snakeskin band, and the narrow hatchet face beneath. The other was moon-faced, button-nosed, with a mean squint and unshaven whiskers so tow-yellow they seemed no more than a whitish sheen against his cheeks. Him, too, Troy Holden remembered from that night in the Montana House, looking on while he faced Luke Bartell.

They had guns belted at their waists, in their saddle boots. They were looking down at Yance Kegley, who had just emerged from the stable with a wheelbarrow-load for the manure pile. One look, and Kegley had snatched up his rifle from where it leaned against a doorpost. He stood, head bared in the weak spring sunlight, the weapon leveled and ready.

The breed ignored the rifle. Holden heard him saying heavily, 'I see you made it through the winter, old man. Like a bear in a hole, or something.'

Kegley's answer was crisp and shaking with some emotion. 'Cut the palaver! I know why you come here, I guess!'

'Oh?' Wasco cocked his narrow head on one side. 'There ain't all that much to know.'

'That's what you say!' Kegley gave a snort, shaking his head like a baited bull. 'I reckon maybe Luke Bartell didn't send the pair of you on purpose to kill me!'

At that, the towhead threw back his head

and a hoot of laughter shook his shoulders. 'Oh, hell!' he retorted when he could speak. 'As if that's all we had to do with our time! We just seen your place, and dropped by. We was sent out to check on the grass, higher up—Luke's gonna be needing plenty of summer feed, now that he's got him a ranch and is bringing in the beef to stock it.'

Wasco nodded curtly, his eyes expressionless. 'That's how it is. You got no quarrel with us, old man. Put up the rifle.'

'Sure!' old Yance retorted. 'You'd like me to do that. Give you a chance maybe to get me in the back!'

The grin faded from the blond rider's face; an angry flush of color began to spread beneath the pale sheen of beard. 'If he'd wanted you killed, do you reckon Luke Bartell would have had to send *two* of us—to take care of one half-witted cripple? Hell, I'd step on you like I would a bug!'

Goaded too far, Yance Kegley cursed and the rifle in his hands snapped up as if he meant to take a shot at the towhead. But Wasco was too quick for him. A jab of the spur sent the breed's roan horse lunging forward, directly at the man on the ground. Too late, Kegley tried to veer out of the way. A muscled shoulder struck him solidly. He lost the rifle and stumbled into the wheelbarrow of manure, toppling it as the gimp leg gave under him and he fell headlong in the mud.

The old man let out a yell. He scrambled to his feet again, but without the rifle, and stood dripping muddy ooze as he watched the horsemen warily closing in on him.

The breed said to his companion, 'Put a rope on him, Starke. Looks like we might have to teach the sonofabitch a lesson.'

'No!' Troy Holden spoke from where he stood a dozen feet away. 'Forget the rope. Both of you—get your hands up!'

Suddenly everything stopped. The towhead, Starke, had already begun taking down the coil from his saddle; he paused and, like his companion, turned to stare at this man who had appeared out of nowhere.

Holden stared back, across the leveled barrel of the gun. He let it swing slightly, its muzzle moving from one rider to the other. 'You haven't raised them!' he pointed out, in warning. Slowly, two pairs of hands groped upward.

Starke was first to find his voice, in a tone of disbelief. 'It's the dude! By God, if it ain't!'

'Surprised to see me?' Holden suggested, his jaw tight. 'Or just surprised to see me *alive*?'

Whatever expression had been in Wasco's dark face withdrew, now, behind a stolid mask. 'We don't exactly know what that's supposed to mean, Holden.'

'Don't you? You didn't have reason to think I might be lying somewhere with a bullet in my back? Or, as much of me as the wolves would have left!'

Imperturbably, Wasco retorted, 'Far as anyone could have guessed, you'd took Luke Bartell's hint and decided to clear the hell out of this country—while the clearing was good. What else would we think?'

The answer Holden might have made was lost as Yance Kegley, with a scream of rage, bent and snatched up his fallen rifle. Whirling on his crippled leg he brought the weapon up for a shot at the man who had dumped him in the mud, but just in time Holden thrust out his left hand and deflected the rifle barrel, shoving it down hard. When the gun went off the bullet plowed into the earth just in front of Wasco's horse. Both animals reacted to the roar of the rifle, acting up and raising gouts of melt water; for a moment the riders had their hands full bringing them under control.

Troy Holden was busy, too, handling the furious old man who was bawling curses and trying to wrest free of Holden's grip on his rifle. Finally Holden had no choice but to take the weapon from him; holding it by the barrel, the six-shooter in his other hand, he told Bartell's men, 'I suggest the two of you get out of here. Now!'

Wasco settled his roan with a savage jerk at the spade bit. When he looked at Holden there was anger in his smoky eyes, but also a certain grudging respect. He said gruffly, 'It appears we got some news for Luke. But if you got good sense, mister, you won't ride into Kettle Creek Valley. There's nothing for you there. Nothing but maybe a bullet!'

Holden's mouth twisted. 'The bullet's already been tried,' he answered. 'And it didn't do the job . . . Now, go on!'

Wasco looked at the six-gun pointed at his chest. He shrugged, and turned his horse. A nod to Starke, and the two of them spurred out of the yard and across the meadow. The drum of hooves echoed from rock faces as they took the dim horse track that led toward lower country.

CHAPTER NINE

Turning to Kegley, Troy Holden offered him the rifle and the old man snatched it from him; he held it in both shaking hands, his body stiff and his arms trembling with thwarted rage. 'Why did you do it?' he cried hoarsely. 'Why'd you stop me, gaddamn you? I'd of killed that breed, wasn't for you!'

'His gun was in the holster. It would have been murder.'

'What the hell do I care? No more'n he deserves. The other one, too. Called me a half-witted cripple . . .'

The muscles of his whole face worked; his lips trembled, his eyes looked out of their

81

sockets with a wild glitter that Holden had seen there before, and that had made him doubt the man's sanity. Holden took a slow breath and said calmly, 'Go ahead and be mad at me. I owe you too much to resent it—but, I think perhaps the time has come for me to leave. I should have gone before.'

'Damn right!' But having said that, Kegley calmed. He looked down at his own soaked and mudstained clothing, and said with a shrug, 'Good thing for me you didn't, though, I guess—you saved me from a bad time, just now. A beating, or worse.'

'It may be I only postponed it. Those two could be back.'

'They'll meet a bullet, if they do—next time, I'll be ready!' The old man added, 'Far as I'm concerned, anything you might have owed me is squared. But now your enemies know you're alive, I'd as soon you cleared out before they come here again looking for you.'

Holden nodded. 'I'll pack my belongings.'

'I doubt we'll be bothered tonight.' Kegley squinted at a gray cloud sheet edging across the sky, bringing a premature dusk. 'Could be a storm, in that—though, it's likely not cold enough for snow. You might as well wait till morning.'

'That makes sense,' Troy Holden agreed. 'Tomorrow, then—and I know you'll be glad to get rid of me!'

And the old man didn't offer to deny it . . .

The storm came in, and by daylight had settled into intermittent squalls of windlashed rain, falling out of a low and slaty sky. Through this—still wearing Yance Kegley's canvas windbreaker, with the converted Smith & Wesson in his pocket—Troy Holden rode the bay horse down toward Kettle Creek. And as he rode, knowing the long period of waiting and convalescence was ended, a tightness began to swell within him. He didn't need the spot of ache low in his back, that the damp chill worked at relentlessly, to remind him what could happen to a man who rode these trails.

Still, it hardly seemed the kind of day for an ambush. Nobody in his right mind would want to be hunkered on his heels under a bush, rifle across his knees, rain dribbling off the brim of his hat and down the neck of his slicker, and turning his cigarette into a sodden mass even as he smoked it. Holden pushed on, and the bay's hide began to steam in the continuing drizzle.

Riding was tiring work, in such weather. Scudding clouds hid the upward peaks, and there was an erratic, tumbling wind that came in spurts to whip at a man's clothing and push him around in his saddle. But now he dropped into a shallow sidecanyon, carved by one of the streams that fed into Kettle Creek, and its walls shut away some of the wind. Here there was grass, and tight-rolled buds about to explode into leaf on bushes and scrub cottonwood; the willows along the stream were so bright red they nearly seemed to glow. Only a few ragged banks of snow were left melting under the rain. In the relative quiet he thought he heard cattle bawling, somewhere ahead, and he caught a whiff of woodsmoke.

Rocks and brush fell away and a flat opened in front of him, with a small holding of shag-pelted cattle feeding and horsemen working them. He saw the source of the smoke—a fire burning on the streambank, a tarp stretched over it to keep off the weather. Nearby a chuckwagon stood, its horse team staked out and tearing at the new grass. Bare-headed in the thin rain, a man was using an ax to chop a downed log into firewood. He stopped his work and straightened, scowling, as Holden rode up.

Trying to work in a wet camp would make any man savage-tempered, Holden thought. Reining in, he remarked sympathetically, 'Not a very good day for it, is it?'

'Ain't nothing good about this!' the other retorted, and squinted suspiciously as a gust of wet wind swept smoke between them. If he had ever seen Holden, he plainly failed to recognize him now.

'What oufit is this?'

'Rockin' Chair,' the man answered, naming Morgan Peters' brand. 'And *you* don't belong to it!' Ax in hand, he sent his stare past Holden, checking to see if he had others with him or came alone. 'Whoever you are,' he declared flatly, 'this ain't where you're supposed to be!'

84

Holden didn't answer. Instead, he turned his head as a trio of riders came jingling toward them from yonder where cattle were being worked and branded. It was Morgan Peters himself, in the lead; close behind him, Holden recognized the Rocking Chair foreman—a slab-lean, black-haired man named Ed Dewhurst. It almost amused him to see how Morgan Peters jerked suddenly straight in the saddle, his eyes widening in astonishment.

'Hello, Morgan,' he said.

The rancher might have seen a ghost. He shook his head slowly, and put up a hand and pulled it across his face and mouth in a bewildered gesture. *'You!'* he exclaimed. 'Where did you come from?' He added, scowling, 'And what the hell has happened to you? You look like the devil. Thinner by twenty pounds since the last time I laid eyes on you!'

'Could be. I've fought a bout with a couple of rifle bullets, since that night last fall. And I didn't win by too wide a margin, at that.'

Words started to tumble from Morgan's mouth. They turned into a bewildered stammer, and he shook his head and tried again. 'Light down, and let's get out of this rain where we can be halfway comfortable. I've got to hear this from the beginning!'

They turned their horses over to the ax-handler and ducked underneath the tarp, where Dewhurst joined them. 'You know my foreman, don't you?' Peters asked by way of

85

introduction. As they hunkered by the fire, the cook brought tin cups and filled them from the big camp pot. Morg Peters produced a bottle, with which he laced the coffee, telling Holden, 'The last time I offered you a drink you turned me down. But a day like this, a man can use a little something to take the chill off.'

Holden was glad enough to agree. He drank, welcoming the spread of warmth the whiskey and boiling coffee put through him. And sitting crosslegged with the drizzling rain tapping its fingers on the stretched tarp overhead, he told in detail the story of his ambushing.

Morgan Peters listened with a scowl and thoughtfully pursed lips. 'You never got any kind of look at whoever shot you?' he demanded. At Holden's shake of head the rancher shrugged. 'Too bad—it might have made a difference. More likely not though, the way things stand.' He drained the last of his coffee-and-whiskey, shook out the grounds into the fire. 'How much do you know of what's been happening down here on the Creek, these past months?'

Grimly Holden said, 'I heard Luke Bartell had helped himself to my ranch.'

'That's exactly what he did! Simply rode in with his crew and took over. No one knew what to do about it. You'd vanished, overnight. All kinds of rumors were going around: That you'd been killed, that Bartell had scared you into running, that he'd closed a legitimate deal and held your bill of sale to prove it.

'I sent my brother down to the county seat, to talk to his boss and check the recorder's office—he could find no record of a sale or transfer of title. Still, lacking a complaint from an aggrieved party, the sheriff didn't figure there was anything for him to do. For all anybody could prove otherwise, Bartell and his crowd were your welcome guests and had every right to be there. And they *do* have possession; hereabouts, that's a good nine-tenths of such law as we've got.'

Troy Holden said, 'Then it's up to Kettle Creek. Just what are you people doing?'

'You can see what we're doing,' Morgan Peters answered roughly. 'I'm not the only rancher that's got his crew in the field, making spring gather six weeks ahead of the normal time. Jim Ells and Bob Thatcher have thrown their crews in with mine. With a man like Bartell for a neighbor, we want our herds counted and the new stuff under our own brands, as early as possible. No use laying temptation in Bartell's way!'

'He might want more from you than a few calves,' Holden warned. 'Yesterday a pair of his men showed up at Yance Kegley's place and said they were checking grass. I gather that Luke Bartell is bringing in outside beef to stock Crown, now that he has possession—and that he means to help himself to as much of your summer graze as he needs, to put it on.'

Morgan Peters stared as though stunned by this news. Beside him the foreman, Ed Dewhurst, swore savagely. Peters, finding his voice, exclaimed huskily, 'I wonder if that's really his game—a squeeze-out! Us Kettle Creek men are willing enough to share our hill range with any reasonable neighbor. But if someone like Bartell moves onto it and starts grabbing and holding . . .' He shook his head, rubbed a rope-scarred hand across his face. Leaving the thought unfinished he said tiredly, 'Well, reckon I better get back to branding.'

He tossed his empty cup into the nearby wreckpan, preparing to heave himself to his feet. Troy Holden said, 'Wait!' And as the older man looked at him: 'There's a side to this thing that we haven't discussed—something Luke Bartell may have lost sight of.'

Peters settled back, probing his face with a narrow look. 'What are you getting at?'

'This.' From an inner pocket he took a bulky envelope and tapped it on his knee. 'I happened to have this in my coat pocket that night I was shot, since I had been expecting to meet George Lunceford in town and close a deal for Crown. It contains the deed, my identification as inheritor—every document I need to prove myself the owner of record. Without it, Luke Bartell hasn't a leg to stand on. *With* it, I can force your sheriff to move whether he wants to or not—or if he won't, then go over his head to the governor and let him know how property rights are being enforced in this part of his State!'

Peters sat a little straighter, a new interest kindled in the glance he exchanged with his foreman. 'Now, there,' he admitted slowly, 'you might have something! Though I can't see Bartell letting a piece of paper get in his way. He'll never give in without a fight—I can promise you that.'

'If things come to a fight, what about you Kettle Creek men? Will you be in it?'

The rancher didn't immediately respond. The thickets of his brows were pulled down in thought as he dug for papers and tobacco sack and expertly spun up a cigarette, seeming to concentrate more than need be on the familiar job his fingers were doing. Finally he said, 'I just can't give you an easy answer, Holden. It might depend on how the fight shaped up—it might depend on a lot of things. For one, it's not realistic to expect a thirty-a-month cowhand would put his life on the line, for the sake of a mere riding job.'

'Meaning, that you can't count on your crews?'

Snapping a match on his thumbnail, Morgan Peters glanced across his shoulder at a rider walking his horse toward the wagon camp through the thin rain. The rancher nodded toward him and the cigarette bobbed between his lips as he said, 'Here's someone it might help for you to talk to . . .'

There was something vaguely familiar about the man, though a rubber poncho made him shapeless and his head was tilted forward as he rode. Troy Holden ducked out from under the tarp, Peters and Dewhurst behind him. He stood waiting, and the oncoming horseman finally lifted his head and he got a view of his face. 'Why, it's Sam Riggs!'

Morgan Peters confirmed it. 'He's riding for me now, since the takeover at Crown . . .'

Stepping forward, Holden reached up a hand toward the man in the saddle. 'Sam! I'm glad to see you.'

The ex-foreman of Crown ranch pulled to a stop. He turned and looked at Holden. And Holden got the shock of his life.

He had never seen such a change in a man. Sam Riggs had seemed, before, almost ageless; now his unshaven cheeks were slack and white-stubbled, sagging as though all the hard years had caught up with him. There were deep lines from nose to mouth corners that Holden didn't remember, and the mouth had none of its old firmness. One eye—the left one—drooped nearly shut and all he could see of it was an eerie half-moon of white.

There was, in this broken old man in the saddle, hardly any likeness to his old friend, the peppery ranch manager who had argued so fiercely against the decision to sell Crown. Not appearing to see the outstretched hand, he laid both his own upon the saddlehorn and leaned his weight on them. For a moment Holden thought the man didn't even recognize him; but then he spoke, in a dull and lifeless voice. 'Holden. Thought we'd seen the last of you. Thought you'd run, for good.'

Slowly, Holden let his arm fall. A surge of temper rose and quickly died, killed by his puzzlement and alarm at what he saw in that other face. Trying to spark some sign of the old fire in it, he said, 'What happened to me doesn't matter. The important thing is, we're going to get Crown back.'

No response in the slack features or in the dull stare of that one eye. Sam finally stirred his shoulders, in a movement that could scarcely even be called a shrug. 'You think so?' he muttered. 'Good luck! If you manage, I hope you get a good price for it.'

He nudged the horse with a heel and sent it on to the picket line. Troy Holden pivoted slowly to watch the old fellow go. Big Morgan Peters moved up beside him.

'What in the name of God is the matter with him?' Holden demanded, aghast.

'You're looking at a whipped man,' the rancher said bluntly. 'When Bartell's crowd rode onto Crown, and told your crew to pack their sougans and drift, Sam Riggs wanted to give them an argument. So they worked him over. Seab Glazer, and that breed they call Wasco—they was particularly eager. They used everything on him, including their gun barrels and their boots. When they were finished they piled him on his horse and took him to the boundaries of the ranch and set him adrift.

'One of the boys found and brought him in, and Callie took on the job of patching him together again. I didn't honestly think he'd pull through. They'd busted him up bad, inside, and they injured that one eye permanent. But the worst damage was to his spirit. You remember the man he was before; well, you've just seen what they left of him . . .'

Troy Holden was having a hard time with his breathing; his chest felt constricted, and angry spasms shook him as he saw Sam Riggs dismounting from his horse now, with the uncertain movements of an old and beaten man.

Morgan Peters was still talking: 'Callie pulled him over the worst of it—I'm real proud of her, for the time and the care she gave him. Once he was on his feet again—at least, as much as he'll ever be—I offered him a job with my crew. Hell, I couldn't do less for a man I've liked and worked with and respected for as long as I've known Sam Riggs! It's a fact he ain't really much use to me, but at least he's got his self-respect. I wouldn't want to have him turning into a barfly, in some cowtown saloon like the Montana House.

'Still, if he was meant for an object lesson, then I reckon Bartell got what he aimed for. Because, I've seen other punchers take a look at what was done to him, and it turns them mighty quiet. And you maybe can't blame them.'

'And that's what you meant,' Troy Holden broke in, 'when you warned me not to count on them in a fight. After seeing Sam, I can understand. I'll remember.'

There seemed little more to say, and he was restless to ride on. The man who had taken his horse was sent to fetch it. In the saddle, Holden paused for a last question. 'How's Callie? She and Jim Ells get married yet?'

Mention of the girl put a coolness between them, reminding of an earlier argument. Peters' thick brows lowered a little and he said carefully, 'Not yet.'

'Just wondered,' Holden said, and reined away from the camp and headed on toward the flat, knowing Morgan Peters watched him go.

CHAPTER TEN

Somehow, as he rode on through the continuing rain, he could not erase the pathetic picture of old Sam Riggs, nor rid himself of the grinding anger that rose each time he thought of what had been done to the loyal Crown foreman. The Kettle Creek ranchers themselves—men like Morgan Peters—had good economic reasons for standing up to Luke

93

Bartell; but Sam Riggs had acted out of nothing but blind loyalty to the brand he rode for, and he had been cruelly repaid. Having seen what had been done to him, Troy Holden knew now there could be no settlement with Bartell that didn't include some element of revenge for Sam.

For the first time, he realized, he was thinking of this business in other terms than the purely selfish one of getting back what had been stolen from him . . .

Where this tributary he had been following broke out of the pines and rushed in a tumble of miniature rapids to pour into Kettle Creek itself, he struck the main valley road. It followed the creek, keeping to a bench above the water but dropping down on occasion to ford it and reach easier grades upon the farther bank. Perhaps it was an illusion but spring seemed further advanced, here in the valley itself. The cottonwoods were beginning to shake out the fresh green of leaves; somewhere behind the leaden, weeping sky, Holden heard a lonely music of wild geese, making north toward Canada.

At the first of the crossings, where the creek sang over a pebbled bottom, he let the bay walk its forefeet into the water and have rein-length to drink. And sitting the saddle, with rain peppering the sliding water, he all at once had an uncanny sensation that other eyes were watching him.

Irritated with himself, he tried to shrug the feeling aside but it persisted so strongly that he scowled and dropped a hand into the pocket of his coat, to touch the gun he carried there. Slowly he lifted his head and ran a look about him, not sure what he was hunting for. He saw nothing, and was ready to blame the tightness of his nerves when the bay suddenly jerked up its head, water dripping in a spray as it snorted and tossed its mane and looked in the direction of a clump of timber on the opposite bank, a few yards upstream.

Troy Holden glanced in that direction, and discovered the pair of horsemen sitting motionless in the shadow of the branches. He saw the saddle gun one of them held, its muzzle carelessly trained on him, and he froze.

The man with the rifle was Seab Glazer; the redheaded gunman called above the murmur of the water: 'All right Holden! Keep coming—right over here to us.'

As Holden hesitated, with the reins tight-gripped until the cold leather ground into his palm, Glazer urged his own horse forward down the bank. A low-hung pine branch hung in his way and he tilted his head slightly, so that the crown of his sweated range hat could clear it. Slight as the movement was, it nevertheless caused the muzzle of the rifle to swing briefly off its target. And Holden gave the bay a kick and a desperate wrench of the reins, in an effort to pull the bay around.

The swiftness of the current was his undoing. The bay tried to turn too fast and in too narrow a space; its hooves slipped and it started to go to its knees. It fought back with a great splashing and rattling of the smooth rounded stones of the creekbed. And in that wildly lunging instant the rifle on the far bank let go.

The bullet hummed past the bay's ear like an angry bee. The horse squealed in terror, rearing, and its legs swept from under it. Man and mount went down.

Holden felt the saddle go from under him and the reins slip from his hand, and icy water closed over his head. An iron shoe struck his shoulder, a numbing blow—it could have crushed his skull, just as easily. It was this terrifying thought that set him struggling to escape the peril of the frightened horse thrashing too close beside him.

He struck the shallow bottom with his shoulders, came up blinded and gasping with water streaming from nose and mouth. He slipped and almost went under again, but caught his footing. Waist-deep in the current, he mopped streaming hair out of his eyes and caught a glimpse of the bay buck-jumping away from him, plunging up the farther bank.

For the moment Holden was powerless to do anything but stand doubled over, coughing the water out of his lungs. When he finally lifted his head, it was to see Glazer and the other man sitting their horses at the edge of the creek and

96

grinning with open amusement. 'By God,' the redhead declared, 'if that wasn't as neat a piece of saddlework as I've seen in a coon's age!'

'I'd of thought it was kind of a chilly day for a swim,' the other Bartell man said.

'You never know about these dudes. Some of 'em are pretty tough.' Abruptly, then, humor died in Glazer's face, leaving it hard and dangerous. He gestured with the barrel of the rifle. 'Come out of there, bucko. Hurry up!' And to his companion: 'Catch up his bronc.'

While the second rider spurred off after it, Troy Holden waded to shore. The muzzle of the rifle resting on Glazer's lap followed him at every step; as he came out of the water, the redhead swung a leg over and stepped down to meet him. Holden could only submit and let the man run a hand over his streaming garments.

Glazer found the six-gun quickly enough and confiscated it, shoving it away behind his pants belt. Still searching, he discovered the manila envelope in another pocket and thumbed open the flap, while Holden tried to conceal his start of alarm. Whether or not he had any idea what it contained, Glazer apparently decided this was worth further study and he pocketed the envelope, afterward stepping back a pace to eye the prisoner narrowly.

'I didn't really know whether to believe it yesterday,' he grunted, 'when we heard you were still around. I thought sure we'd seen the

97

last of you. Well, I got an idea now you're going to wish we had! After Luke's had what he wants from you, we're gonna take up the little matter of you trying to get tough with me, that night in the Montana House . . .'

Holden made no attempt to answer. He had been wet enough before, thanks to the needling rain, and after his ducking he was soaked through. Now the cold was getting through him, to the bone. He had lost his hat and the hair was plastered to his skull; he put up a hand and shoved it back from his eyes, and then the other rider was back leading the bay by its reins.

'Mount up,' Seab Glazer ordered.

'Where are you taking me?'

'Where'd you think? To Luke, of course . . .'

And so this was his return to Crown ranch— a sodden figure, bracketed by his captors' mounts, trying to contain the spasms of shaking chill that ran through him as the wind hit with icy impact. His shoulder hurt where the bay kicked it and so did that spot of ache low in his back—his constant reminder of the rifle slug that had nearly crippled him, months ago. He looked at the rifle in Seab Glazer's saddle scabbard, and wondered if it might have been the same weapon.

They followed the river, coming at last to the feeder gulch where a wooden sign indicated the side road to Crown. By this time the rain had slacked off and nearly ceased, though the mounting wind kept the day miserable and the low clouds scudding overhead. There would be an early dusk, still a matter of hours ahead.

They took the side road, and presently passed beneath the high gateway with the brand burned on a slab of wood that swung wildly in the wind, from the crossbar. A little later, twisting past a stand of aspen mixed with pine, the familiar road brought Troy Holden and his captors in on the headquarters buildings of the ranch Luke Bartell had stolen from him.

Crown had scarcely been a working outfit, running a minimum crew and no more than a token beef herd, while waiting for Vern Holden to decide how he meant to develop it. Nevertheless Sam Riggs, as manager, had done what he could on limited funds and had taken pride in keeping the physical plant—house and barn and corrals and allied structures—in top condition: Fences taut, paint constantly renewed, shingled roofs and siding intact. Now it seemed to Holden, as they rode in, that he could already see signs of deterioration in the few months of Bartell's occupancy. The door of a tack shed, broken off its hinges and simply leaning against the opening with no attempt to repair it, was a small thing that told a great deal. Somehow it sharpened Holden's anger as much as anything he had seen yet.

The buildings lay along the foot of a rim, with tongues of pine and aspen in new leaf running up the folds of the hill behind. Someone came to the bunkhouse door and watched the three ride by, and when they were within a few yards of the main building Luke Bartell himself strode out onto the porch.

He came to the edge of the steps and halted, arms akimbo, the wind plucking at his coat and lifting the thick mop of black hair upon his head. Seab Glazer told him, 'I brought you something.'

'Looks like you brought me a drowned rat.'

Holden found it humiliating that, despite all his efforts, he still could not prevent the shudders of chill from shaking him. Bartell saw and the heavy moustache lifted above a grin of cruel amusement, though the eyes remained agate-hard and devoid of humor. 'Mister,' he said, 'you're a hard man to get rid of.'

And a harder one to kill, Holden would have answered in defiance, but his lips and tongue felt too stiff to form the words. He merely stared back and Glazer said, 'He wasn't too damned hard to catch.'

Bartell turned away, throwing an order across his shoulder: 'Fetch him in.'

When he stepped down, Holden nearly went to his knees; his feet and legs were like chunks of ice, and the muscles threatened to cramp. He set his jaw, forcing life into his limbs. But then Glazer gave him a shove toward the door Bartell had left open, and he had to grab at the frame to keep from stumbling.

100

Inside, welcome warmth met him—the one thing he could see at first was the roaring leap of flames in the wide stone fireplace. He walked directly to the fire and spread his hands to it, soaking up warmth, feeling it spread through the stiffness in his limbs. At once a steaming odor of wet wool began to rise from his clothing, mingling with other smells of liquor, tobacco, and sweat.

Only now did he become aware of the half dozen men scattered about the room, some sprawled comfortably in leather-slung armchairs or on the big horsehair sofa. One— it was the breed, Wasco—leaned against the wall with his arms folded and a keen interest in his narrow hatchet face as he watched Holden.

No one interfered with him. Seab Glazer was telling of the capture, and the ludicrous spectacle of the dude falling with his horse into the creek lost nothing in the way he told it; it brought contemptuous snickers from his listeners, which Holden, peering into the fire, ignored. But he turned as he heard Glazer saying, 'I took this off of him, Luke. Figured it was something you'd want to see.'

Bartell, seated now on a corner of the big oak center table, took the manila envelope Glazer handed him. River water had not had time to get at the contents; Bartell dug them out and leafed through them. Eyes thoughtful, he shoved the papers back and laid the envelope on the table beside him, and looked at Holden, idly swinging one booted leg.

Holden returned his stare. A lamp in a wall bracket had been lighted against the dull light of the afternoon, and it showed him what had been done to this house by its new occupants.

They hadn't been easy on it. The floor was actually littered with trash and, especially in the vicinity of the fire-place, was freely spattered with gobbets of dried tobacco juice. Some accident had happened to one of the windows; a broken pane was masked with cardboard and the curtain hung in shreds. Floor and furniture alike were generously scarred with spur marks—the man lounging in the chair by the table had now scooted around and cocked one boot upon the edge of the mahogany where he rocked it idly back and forth, spur rowel carving a trough deep into the fine wood.

Troy Holden deliberately took his eyes from this destruction.

Bartell said, 'I didn't rightly know if I believed it, yesterday, when Starke and Wasco said they'd run into you up at old Yance Kegley's.'

'I can understand that,' Holden replied grimly. 'It looks as though someone didn't quite do his job with a rifle.'

A faint scowl etched its crease between the outlaw's brows. Not directly answering the charge, he said, 'Well, now, most people here on the Kettle have been taking it for granted you done the smart thing and cleared out when

I told you. I'm afraid you showing up again, like this, wasn't quite so smart after all.'

'Smart or not, remains to be seen.'

'You think so?' Cold contempt turned Bartell's voice crisp as he indicated his silently listening crew. 'Look around you, mister. Do you really think there's a single damn thing you can do to me?'

Troy Holden followed the gesture, considering the menace that surrounded him. He drew a breath, and hoped he sounded more confident than he felt. 'This isn't the Dark Ages. It's 1893! You can thumb your nose at law and order if you want to; but even in this forgotten part of the world, sooner or later they're going to catch up with you, Bartell!'

'Not with me,' the outlaw retorted flatly. 'Because, you see, I *am* a smart man! I always know just what I'm doing. If you don't think so, here's something you might take a look at.'

He eased off the edge of the table, rang his spurs across the floor to a rolltop desk that stood against one wall of the room. From a pigeonhole he took a folded paper, returned with it and handed it to Holden. Curious, the latter looked it over and saw it was a bill of sale to Crown Ranch—land, stock, and buildings.

The signature was his own.

Holden stared at the writing, and his head lifted and his angry stare met Bartell's. 'A forgery!' he snapped.

'And a damned good one,' the outlaw agreed

blandly, 'if I do say it myself. Don't bother tearing it up,' he added quickly, and took the paper back from Holden's fingers. 'Only put me to the bother of having it to do again.

'You left me several good samples in the desk to work from,' Bartell went on pleasantly. 'And now you've been good enough to drop these in my lap.' He picked up from the table the papers Glazer had taken from the prisoner. 'This title deed, with the assignment duly made over, should give me all the legal claim I'll ever need.' Smiling crookedly beneath the heavy moustache, he slipped the sheaf of papers back into the envelope. Troy Holden, with darker feeling than he would have wanted to show, watched the manila envelope disappear into an inner pocket of the outlaw's corduroy coat.

Bartell took whiskey bottle and glass from the table, poured himself a drink. Leaning his hips once more against the table's edge, he pointed the glass at Holden and said crisply, 'So now you know the score—and some other people are going to learn it, too. I'm making changes around here. This ranch was never given a chance to amount to much; but from now on there's going to be one important outfit on the Kettle, and it's gonna be Crown. And, that means Luke Bartell!'

Holden said, 'I didn't really think you intended standing still. Your men told me, yesterday, you already had them out scouting summer range.'

'That's right.' Bartell took a drag at the whiskey, his obsidian stare considering Holden shrewdly. 'As it happens I've got a thousand new head of beef on the way, should be getting in tomorrow maybe. And that's only a start.'

'A start, you mean, at crowding every other brand off the hills and out of the valley!'

The outlaw shrugged. 'That doesn't concern you, does it?'

'And just what do you imagine I'll be doing, while it's going on?'

'If you don't watch your step, you could be lying under a cutbank somewhere,' Bartell answered bluntly. 'With dirt in your face.'

Holden said, 'I suppose the second time, you imagine you can get the job done.'

It was a long moment before Bartell answered. He finished his drink slowly while his eyes studied the prisoner above the rim of the glass, his expression veiled and unreadable. Finally Bartell set the empty glass on the table and said crisply, 'I won't even pretend to know what you're talking about, mister. I do know I'm getting a little tired of you. I still got no use for dudes, and for you in particular!'

The rest of the outlaws had heard all this without any comment or interference. Now Seab Glazer shifted his boots and said gruffly, 'Why waste palaver? Just tell me what you want done with him.'

Bartell rubbed a thumbnail across his jaw. He said, finally, 'What you did to that other stubborn fool—that Sam Riggs—seems to have been effective. We'll try the same dose, again.'

Glazer's eyes narrowed. He said doubtfully, 'You sure about this? You don't want him dead?'

'Riggs was about twice the man he is, by my estimation,' Bartell answered with a shrug. 'It was just a fluke, him getting the best of you that night in the Montana House. And I imagine you'll see to it that by the time you get through with him now, there won't be enough left to give us any more trouble.' He looked at the breed, leaning impassively against the wall. 'You want a part of this?'

'Yeah.' Wasco pushed to a stand, a gleam of pleasure lighting his smoky eyes. 'Yeah, I want a piece. I got a little score of my own to settle.'

Bartell nodded. 'You know what to do. Take him to the edge of Crown grass, and give him what you gave Sam Riggs and set him adrift. Make sure he don't ever want to try coming back . . .'

CHAPTER ELEVEN

They must have been inside the ranch house longer than it seemed, for when they emerged it had stopped raining. This, at least, was welcome. Holden had managed to dry out after a fashion, standing in front of the log blaze, but

106

his clothing still held dampness and the searching wind quickly got to him. Now as he climbed stiffly to the saddle, at Glazer's curt order, and rode away from the ranch house with the redhead and the breed flanking his horse, the clouds overhead actually showed signs of breaking. A dazzle of late afternoon sunlight marbled their blank gray surface.

Glazer didn't set the same course by which they'd arrived at Crown; the main road was probably too well traveled, and he'd want more privacy for what he had in mind. Instead, the three rode directly south, over valley grass that was chopped up by tributary ravines and broken by tongues of timber. Troy Holden debated trying to make a break and hit for the cover of some of those inviting trees, but each time he gave it up; something told him his guards would be waiting for him to make such a mistake.

Seab Glazer appeared to be enjoying himself; he even struck up a tuneless whistling through his teeth that grated on the prisoner's tense nerves. Once, the redhead broke off long enough to tell Wasco, 'Damn good thing you brought a rope. I forgot to.'

The breed grunted something. Glazer asked the prisoner, 'I reckon you know why we need a rope?'

Holden shook his head. Glazer gave a snort of laughter. 'When we get through with you, and turn you loose, you ain't gonna be in any shape to set that saddle. We're gonna have to *tie* you on!' A moment later he pulled rein and told the breed, 'We might as well get at this.'

Wasco dismounted without comment. Seab Glazer gave Holden a command which he thought of disobeying; but he had no choice, and with reluctance he stepped down while the redhead watched him carefully. When Glazer was off, the breed took all three horses and anchored them to a fallen pine.

They stood in rank wire grass, on ground that was sodden from rain and snow melt; a multitude of tiny green toads slithered away from Glazer's boots as he walked to face the prisoner. A grin of evil pleasure lifted the man's upper lip, revealing strong white teeth; piercing blue eyes stabbing at Holden, Glazer deliberately worked the fingers of his right hand—flexing and spreading them, in anticipation.

Staring at the fist, and then at the ice-blue eyes peering at him above slanted cheekbones, Troy Holden remembered Sam Riggs as he had looked after this pair got through with him, and he knew what was in store for him; he very nearly gave way to despair. Seab Glazer took another step and set himself. Somewhere to Holden's left and rear, he could hear Wasco's boots whispering in the wire grass as he came up from tying the horses. For that one moment his enemies were separated, and with a sudden lunge Holden launched himself forward, every ounce of his will and shoulder muscle going into the swing of his fist at the jut of Seab Glazer's jaw.

Apparently the desperate move came, as he had meant it, as a complete surprise. The redhead put up no defense at all, and only at the last instant did he think to save himself by jerking back and tucking his chin under. Holden's fist missed its target but it bounced off Glazer's chest, throwing him off balance. At the same instant Holden's left hand was grabbing for the handle of Yance Kegley's six-shooter, still shoved behind the redhead's belt. His fingers managed to touch the gun. He almost got a grip on it; then Glazer stumbled backward, out of his reach, and something heavy that could only be Wasco's fist struck a clubbing blow at the point where Holden's neck joined the shoulder. Crippling pain smashed through the upper part of his body and he felt himself going down.

Somehow, dazed as he was, he knew that a boot would follow up the blow and when he lit he managed to roll, trying to escape it. So when Wasco drove the kick at his body, he felt it only in a wrench of his clothing as the heavy cowhide just missed his flesh. He was on his face in the wire grass then and he got his hands under him and started to push himself up. A shadow fell across him. He heard Seab Glazer's angry cursing and a hand grabbed his collar and he was hauled up, arms dangling helplessly. A fist smashed him in the face. The very violence of the blow tore his clothing from Glazer's grasp and dropped him onto his side; he lay there, almost as though paralyzed by the crushing blow he had taken. A taste of blood was in his mouth.

Glazer was cursing his companion. 'Damn it, get the bastard on his feet and *hold* him. Give me a fair chance!'

They both had him then, dragging him upright. His arms were seized and hauled roughly behind him. For a moment he found his face pressed flat against Seab Glazer's chest; he caught the gamey smell of the man's clothing. Deliberately he jerked his head up with all the strength he could manage, felt the top of his skull make solid contact with Glazer's jaw. He heard the crunch of the man's teeth clicking together. Glazer stumbled back, letting out a howl that sounded as though he might have bitten his tongue. The thought gave Holden a moment's satisfaction, even though he knew he was likely going to pay for it.

Then hard blows were ripping at him. A cheek was laid open, a fist took him on an ear and set his whole head to ringing. Something slammed into his middle, and to the sledging pain of it the breath gusted through bleeding lips and he tried to go to his knees, both pinioned arms feeling as though they would tear from the sockets.

A gun went off, somewhere. There was a

shout, and the ground carried the drumming jar of horses' hooves. Another shout; he thought a voice was saying, 'Let him go, or I'll aim for somebody's leg!' Abruptly, then, his arms were freed and he sagged limply forward to the ground, onto his face.

Dazed as he was with pain and gulping for the wind that had been knocked out of him, Troy Holden nevertheless managed to raise his head, and had a look at his rescuers. To his astonishment he saw they were Jim Ells and Callie Peters. They had ridden out of the trees some hundred yards distant, the outlaws being so engrossed in what they were doing to Holden they'd let themselves be taken unawares.

Now Holden looked at the gun, still smoking in Ells' hand after the warning shot, and he thought in alarm, *You can't handle both these men!* Luckily, the yellow-haired rancher had sense enough not to try. He saw the pair, overcoming their first surprise, start to drift slightly apart like wolves separating to come at their prey from two directions for the kill. He couldn't cover them both, so he made his choice and dropped his gun muzzle squarely on Seab Glazer. He said, in a voice that shook slightly, 'Tell your friend to unbuckle his gun and drop it. One funny move from him, Glazer, and by God I'll drop *you!*'

The redhead glowered, but he must have recognized that Jim Ells was frightened enough

111

to be dangerous. His mouth twisted and he growled an order at his companion: 'I guess you better do what he says.' Just the same Wasco hesitated—after all, it wasn't his head the gun was pointed at. But Glazer swore at him and, with a shrug, the breed unhooked his belt buckle and let belt and holster fall.

'Now, you,' Ells said, and the redhead followed suit, afterward dropping the gun he'd taken off Troy Holden. His eyes never left Jim Ells as he turned his head and spat blood on the ground from his bitten tongue; his scowl held murder.

Callie Peters leaped down from the saddle, now, ground-reining her pony. She was dressed as Holden was most often used to seeing her—in work clothes, jeans and boots and hickory shirt, with a corduroy jacket and flat-crowned riding hat. She started toward Holden as he climbed to his feet; glad as he was to see her, he waved her away as he said gruffly, 'I'm all right. Just let me have one of those guns.'

Yance Kegley's pistol was the nearest and Callie quickly got it and passed it to him. Ells was herding the outlaws toward the log where their horses were tied. Holden called a quick warning: 'Careful! There's a rifle on one of those saddles!'

'Get rid of it,' the rancher ordered. Sullenly, Glazer slid it from the scabbard and leaned it against the log; afterward, on command, both men whipped their reins free and swung into the saddles.

Glazer, cutting his hating stare back and forth, told the three of them, 'You'll hear more about this!'

'I don't doubt it,' Jim Ells said. To Holden he sounded resigned and apprehensive, though his manner was firm enough. 'But for the time being it ends here. You can come back later to pick up your guns. Now, get out of here and leave us alone!'

Without further argument, the outlaws kicked their horses and the others watched as they rode away, finally vanishing across a shallow rise. Jim Ells looked a little white. He blew out his cheeks and the gun sagged in his hand. 'They've headed toward Crown. Do you suppose they're going for help?'

'We had better not wait to find out,' Holden said grimly. He added, 'I can't begin to thank you for this. They were going to give me what they gave Sam Riggs!'

The rancher shrugged, and slid his gun back into the holster. 'Thank Callie. Butting in was her idea.' Holden could have said that didn't surprise him at all. He imagined Ells resented having to take any part in what had happened.

To an anxious question from the girl, Troy Holden said, 'I'm all right, really. But let's get out of here . . .'

He was already pocketing Kegley's six-shooter, moving stiffly to his waiting horse; his whole body ached in protest. Only after she saw

113

him gain the saddle, would Callie Peters turn to her own.

They all rode easier once they knew they had passed the boundaries of Crown, but they kept on during another silent quarter hour. At last they drew up in a screen of timber where they had a good view of the trail they had left. There was a spring, here, born of melting snow; while Jim Ells kept a watch for pursuit, Troy Holden climbed down from the saddle. He shook his head at Callie, hovering anxiously and eager to help, and instead scooped up the icy water in his hands and bathed the cuts on his face.

His cheek stung like fire; his belly held a deep ache and his shoulder, where Wasco had clubbed him, hurt whenever he moved his arm. But the icy shock of the water helped clear his head. Holden rinsed his bleeding mouth and had a long drink, and mopped his face on a sleeve of his ruined coat. 'They didn't have a chance to do the job they wanted to on me—though I still don't understand how you showed up, just when I needed you.'

Jim Ells explained briefly. 'We learned that you'd been at the roundup fire, and left on the road to Reserve. Callie insisted on riding after you, and at the crossing we saw sign that looked like you might have run into trouble. The tracks led to Crown. We were watching the house when they brought you outside.'

'It wouldn't have gone well,' Holden said, 'if you'd been caught.'

Ells shrugged and looked away. It occurred to Holden that, as it had worked out, to all intents and purposes they *had* been caught. Bartell's men would not forget this afternoon. 'I'm sorry as the devil that the two of you had to get involved,' he said. 'But it was one of the luckiest things ever happened to me!'

Callie stood close beside him, looking up into his face. The horses had fallen to cropping at the thin grass near the spring. There seemed no indication that anyone had followed them from Crown; the late afternoon quiet could hardly have been more peaceful.

All except for the black scowl on Jim Ells face as he watched the girl saying, 'Troy, you don't know how we've wondered—and worried—since that night last fall when you disappeared!' Holden knew Ells' look; he had seen it on the blond rancher before. It was pure, naked jealousy.

Feeling she didn't have his attention, Callie put her hand on Holden's sleeve. 'Pa told me someone tried to—*kill* you!'

'They didn't quite manage.' He looked at her and smiled, though a trifle bleakly.

'You think it was one of Luke Bartell's crowd?' Jim Ells asked.

'That seems rather obvious, doesn't it? When you see who's now sitting on my ranch!'

'Morg says you have the papers to fight him in court, if it comes to that . . .'

That reminded Holden of his loss, and he

115

half raised a hand to his empty pocket and let it fall again. 'There were papers,' he said, 'but Bartell has them now. On top of that, he turns out to be a first class forger! He showed me a bill of sale for Crown, that I would have sworn I had signed myself! Now that he holds the deed and everything else, he can fix things so that fighting him is going to be a very tricky business.'

Callie said fiercely, 'But you're not going to quit!'

'Oh, I'll fight him,' Holden promised, his voice hard. 'But I don't know just at the moment, what with . . .'

They talked a while longer, comparing notes and conjectures, accomplishing little. Finally Holden turned to his horse and checked the cinch and, with one hand on the pommel, said, 'If anyone wants me, I'm riding on to Reserve. It appears I've got some hard thinking to do. There's one other thing,' he added, remembering; and he told them what Luke Bartell had boasted—of a thousand head of seed stock on its way to Kettle Creek, due to arrive perhaps tomorrow. From their expressions, he knew they both saw the seriousness of this.

He said, 'I told Morgan Peters I'd got wind of some such thing; now I have it direct from Bartell himself. It's my guess this herd will only be the first. He's got unlimited sources of stolen cattle—covered by forced bills of sale, of course! He can keep bringing them in, loading the range down with them and pushing his neighbors until something gives way. There's no reason to think he'll quit until he's taken everything in sight.'

The girl seemed shocked beyond speech. Jim Ells, his face thunderous, blurted out, 'But—*why*? What does scum like Bartell want with a ranch and grazing rights? Him and that cutthroat gang of his have never been anything but longriders!'

Troy Holden shrugged. 'Perhaps that's just the point. It could be there's a side to such a man that nobody ever guesses. Perhaps he's decided, all at once, that now he wants respectability.'

'Yeah!' Ells grunted. He drew a breath. 'Well, I'll pass this word—though what anyone can do, is a little more than I see just at the moment. Kettle Creek men ain't ever been called on to do a hell of a lot of fighting.'

'I'm afraid they'll fight now, or they'll end up where I am—with nothing at all!' Holden swung into the saddle. There seemed nothing more to say. He nodded to them both, and turned his horse in the direction of the valley road.

CHAPTER TWELVE

A full moon was rising behind banks of broken cloud as he came into Reserve, making him think of the night last fall when he had ridden into this town with Sam Riggs, to keep his aborted appointment with a buyer for Crown. He felt infinitely older, scarred and bone-weary and wiser to the ways of this land—he thought of how detached and superior he had felt then, to the local people and their problems and knew he had only been naïve.

Luke Bartell had been an education.

Just as on that other night, a stagecoach was making up for its run to railhead. Melcher, the agent, stood talking to the driver and he recognized Holden instantly, as Troy put his horse to the tie rail before the station. Melcher seemed not at all surprised, from which Holden judged that news of his reappearance had preceded him, likely carried by someone from Morgan Peters' roundup camp. 'I got mail for you,' Melcher said, and Holden followed him inside the station where the agent opened a desk drawer and took out a bundle of nearly a dozen envelopes tied with string.

'Some of these came last fall,' he said, 'after you—uh—disappeared. I hadn't made up my mind yet whether to return them, when the passes closed. The rest have been piling up at railhead, all winter long, waiting for the first coach to bring them in.'

Nearly all, Holden saw on thumbing through the envelopes, were from his New York attorney. One or two were marked 'Urgent!' He merely stuffed them into a pocket, thanked the man, and left.

Before anything else, just now, he needed dry clothing. Luckily the store was still open; having given a boy a dollar to take his horse to the livery barn, he went in and bought everything new, from the skin out, settling for whatever the merchant had available—sturdy-looking jeans, flannel shirt, a jacket and hat. He changed in the store's back room, noticing in a mirror that the cuts and swellings resulting from his fight with Glazer and Wasco, while nasty enough, had not left his face in too bad shape after all. Afterward he crossed the street to the restaurant where he ordered dinner and then, having lighted up the first from a new box of tailormades, settled back at last for a look at his mail.

He arranged the letters chronologically, by their postmarks, and ripped open the envelopes and stolidly read his way through the record of a winter of disaster. He found nothing in it that he could not have foreseen, and hadn't already taken for granted. Yet there was a grim finality about seeing everything in black and white. The lawyer had done all he could to protect an absent client's interests; still, with no word from Troy Holden despite his constant letters and his repeated pleas for

119

advice, there had been little enough he could do. And so, slowly at first and then in a sucking rush; everything had gone. While Troy Holden lay on that musty bed in Yance Kegley's cabin, the last of the Holden possessions had been sold from under him.

Except for his horse, the new clothes on his back, the few dollars left in his wallet—and title to a ranch that he was no longer sure he could prove—there was simply nothing. He was a ruined man.

He stubbed out his cigarette and took up the one remaining envelope. It bore no return, nothing but a New York postmark ten days old. It felt too thin to contain a letter. He ripped it open, and a newspaper clipping fell upon the table cloth.

He sat and looked at it, his stare floundering down the narrow column of print: 'The wedding of Beatrice Applegate and Charles Frederick . . . The bride, daughter of socially prominent . . . The groom is a member of the New Haven shipping family, graduate of Yale in the class of . . .' It was all there, down to the last details of the wedding gown and the flowers in the ushers' buttonholes, and yet for a stunned moment Holden was unable to take it in.

Bea—and a man he had not even known was in her circle of friends! Was it something that had been going on all the time, without his hearing a word of it? Or, had it begun only since he left the East, coming to a head during long winter months when she had no word of him? What about all the letters he had written, last fall, and the ones from her he'd waited for so impatiently and never received? Could it be that, even then—?

It didn't matter. It didn't matter a damn!

The waiter brought his plate, just then, and set it before him. Holden looked at the food, and with a shake of his head pushed it aside. He gathered up his mail, crammed it into a pocket; he left money beside the plate, got his hat and stumbled out into the early night. Still dazed, he stood blinking, seeing nothing; then the lights of the Montana House caught his eye. He headed that way, at a long angle across the empty street.

He scarcely bothered to notice if there was anyone else in the big room, blind even to the danger from Luke Bartell's men. Hardly responding to Costello's greeting or noticing the curious look the man gave his battered face, he called for a bottle. He poured a drink, tossed it off and, ignoring the pitcher of water the Irishman set out for him, immediately poured a second shot without a chaser. He scarcely noticed how it stung in the cuts on the inside of his cheek.

Costello said mildly, 'I'd go easy on that stuff, Holden. It's got a kick.'

'Fine,' Holden grunted, and drank and poured again. But then the revulsion of a

121

system untrained to the brutal assault of so much raw alcohol, taken so quickly, hit him and he put the glass down with a shudder.

Seeing this, Costello nodded in sympathy. 'That's better. I heard about what was done to you—I guess the whole town's heard, by now. It's enough to make a man tie one on. But that won't lick Bartell.'

Irritated, Holden moved a hand in a curt dismissal. Costello meant well but he had no idea what he was talking about. He didn't know about Bea Applegate, and Holden wasn't going to discuss her with a bartender; he hadn't hit *that* low.

But enough hard common sense remained to tell him that drinking himself into a stupor would not solve his problem. Angrily he shoved the glass away, so hard that it overturned and rolled across the polished wood. With no more than a reproachful look, Costello righted the glass and used his bar rag to mop up the spilled whiskey.

'Sorry,' Holden grunted, and turned to look at the room.

It was early yet and he was Costello's only customer; but the saloon could have been filled with Bartell riders, and in his blind emotion he would not have seen the danger. Shuddering a little at his own careless stupidity, he drew a breath and forced a grip on himself; but the sense of abysmal emptiness—and the crawling burn of the whiskey—filled him and for a

122

moment he felt he might be sick.

That passed. With clearer thought came a question which, he thought, only Costello might be able to answer. He took another of his machine-rolled cigarettes and lighted it, fighting to keep his hand from trembling, as he shaped his words.

'I take it you have no real love for Bartell,' he said carefully. 'Will you tell me something I want to know—if I promise it won't go any farther, and you won't be held to account for it, ever?'

The Irishman's eyes narrowed. He rubbed the bar with his cloth, as he considered. 'Try me.'

Holden said, 'This is probably asking too much—there's no reason you should remember the night, last fall, when I had my encounter here with Luke Bartell. Still, I'm wondering if by any chance you can tell me which one of Bartell's men might have left soon after I did, that night. Because that had to be the one that followed me, and shot me in the back!'

Costello regarded him for a long moment as though weighing his answer. He shook his head. 'I see your thinking, but I'm afraid you got it wrong. It wasn't any of them.'

Holden stared. 'You must be mistaken!'

'Not a chance. When I got Bartell and his crowd in my place, I don't lose track of them for a minute! There was eight of them here that night, and I particularly remember, after the way you roughed Seab Glazer, I was leery Glazer might take his mad out on my place of business. But nothing much happened. They hung around, drinking and playing poker, till nearly two in the morning; and when they left, they all left together. And in that time, none of that crowd was out of my sight for longer than ten minutes or so at a stretch—mostly, to use the privy out back. I know for certain, it wasn't long enough to have had anything to do with bushwhacking you.'

'But—!' The protest died in a stammer; Troy Holden scowled fiercely at the man, wondering if the two drinks he had taken could have befuddled his thinking.

If not Luke Bartell—or Glazer, or the breed, or any of those others—then it appeared his whole line of thinking on the subject of the ambush was dead wrong. And who, then? It simply didn't make sense!

He remembered suddenly Bartell, and Glazer too, both insisting today they knew nothing about the attempt on his life; it looked as though they could have been telling the truth! But who else did it leave? All at once, like a cold finger touching his spine, the memory came back of Morgan Peters warning him to stay away from Callie; of Jim Ells and his jealous rage, that fateful night, and their short and indecisive battle in the jail office.

Yet this very afternoon, Jim Ells had saved him from a beating, or worse. And as for

Morgan Peters, he surely wouldn't shoot any man in the back! Or, was that really so certain? Now that they thought Holden might be useful to them in their own fight with Bartell, they could have decided it made sense to change their policy and try to keep him alive . . .

Costello was peering at him curiously. 'From the look of you, I'd say I just blowed you clean out of the pond!'

'I won't deny it,' Troy Holden said shortly. 'But I have to thank you for the information.' For a moment he wondered if Costello could be the one who was lying, then for some reason decided otherwise. He had a strong feeling that the Irishman, even if forced to remain more or less neutral, had no use at all for Luke Bartell. Completely bewildered, he shrugged and dug up a bill and dropped it on the counter. 'For the drinks,' he said. 'Including the one I spilled. Whatever I need right now, it plainly isn't liquor. A good night's sleep, maybe.'

Moving rather like a man in a daze, he turned and walked out into the spring evening.

*   *   *

He woke in a hotel bed and lay for a long time staring at the ceiling, where a reflection of morning sun on a rain-puddle in the street below danced and shimmered. All that he had learned, and all that had happened to him yesterday since he rode down from Kegley's

125

shack in the hills, came over him afresh and brought a hopeless feeling of muddle and confusion. The lawyer's letters, and that damned newspaper clipping, lay on a table beside the bed, mocking him with their message of total loss.

When he moved to rise, his whole body seemed a solid ache of protest. Seab Glazer and the breed had been stopped before they could give him the beating they intended to, but they had done well enough.

The reflection of his swollen face in the mirror showed the evidence. Holden fingered his beardstubbled cheek and hoped the barber in this town possessed a gentle hand. He moved about the room, easing some of the soreness out of his muscles, taking his time with dressing. And as he buttoned his shirt he stepped to the window for a look into the street, and thus saw the three riders jogging up the street toward the intersection where the hotel stood.

His hands went suddenly still. He recognized the conical crown and the snakeskin band of Wasco's hat, first of all; then another of the foreshortened figures identified itself as Seab Glazer, and he decided the third looked something like the towhead, Starke, who had been with Wasco at Kegley's place two days ago. He saw them pull rein near the street's opposite corner, catty-cornered from the hotel; he saw them conferring, still in the saddle, and he noticed how they continued to look in his direction.

Holden drew back from the window, not liking this.

He finished dressing quickly, stowed his belongings in his pockets, took the jacket and hat he'd bought last evening and, finally, picked up the converted Smith & Wesson. Weighing it thoughtfully in his hand, he had another look through the window and this time failed to see any of Bartell's men.

It would be hard to say why he felt so strongly their presence in town this morning had something to do with himself. Still, the alarm bells were beating inside him as he left his room, locking the door behind him, and traveled down the faded carpet of the corridor toward the lobby stairs. The gun was in his pocket, but so was his hand.

Starting to descend the steps, he caught the sound of voices and something prompted him to caution. Halting, he dropped to a crouch and now could look down into the lobby, and just make out the one who stood at the desk talking to Sid Bravender. Right enough—it was Starke. He had the desk register turned toward him and he tapped the page with one forefinger while Holden heard him say, too quietly, 'Next time, friend, don't lie to me. Not when I can read for myself!' Bravender stared back, a frightened look on him. Starke pushed the book away and strode out of Holden's line of vision, but his voice rose clearly as he called to someone beyond the street door: 'We were right. He's here . . .'

A step creaked under Holden's weight. Bravender, behind the desk, glanced toward the stairs; when he saw Holden a look of horror seized his face. He flung a pointing hand toward the invisible Starke, while he shook his head in frantic warning. Holden, nodding, simply straightened and faded up the steps; in the upper hall he hesitated, debating his moves. A slight, cold sweat broke out upon his face.

There could be no doubt of it now: Whether actually sent by Luke Bartell, or merely turned loose to settle scores for themselves, the three of them were after Holden, and arrogant enough to come directly into town to find him. If they laid hands on him, he felt, this time they would not settle for a beating.

Voices below, again. It sounded like two men, crossing the lobby in long strides—so, perhaps the third remained outside on the street, in case they might be mistaken and the dude wasn't in his room. Holden retreated before them, moving back through the dim hall. At the rear end of the corridor daylight showed through the glass of an outside door, that opened upon the head of a flight of wooden steps angling toward an alley below. Fortunately the door wasn't locked. He wrenched it open and darted through, just as the tread of heavy boots hit the forward end of

128

the corridor. He could only hope his enemies failed to see the door closing, or catch his shadow silhouetted against the pebbled glass.

He went down the ladder-like steps as swiftly and silently as he could, and now the gun was in his hand.

CHAPTER THIRTEEN

Troy Holden could only wonder about the third man, the one who hadn't entered the hotel. As he dropped down the steps he could feel every muscle tighten and the juices dry out of his mouth, at thought of Seab Glazer—or the breed, perhaps—down there somewhere with a gun already trained on him, dead center, letting him walk into it. But he reached the alley without a challenge. Beyond this rear corner of the hotel lay a cross street, and here he paused for a look to his left, toward the junction with Main.

At once he saw Seab Glazer.

The redhead had taken a stance in the middle of the intersection, where he could watch not only the hotel but the livery barn opposite, as well as the approaches along both arteries. That way he could prevent any chance of Holden's getting to his horse; all he had to do was wait where he was while the pair he had sent into the hotel flushed his quarry out to him.

Holden lifted his gun, wondering if he could get a shot at Glazer. In that same instant, there was the sound behind him of a door violently thrown open. Jerking about, he saw Wasco and the towhead, Starke, emerge at the head of the outside stairs, and he knew he had never fooled them at all. One of the pair gave a shout and a gun's roar filled the alleyway. The bullet missed. Desperately Holden threw a shot up the stairway, hoping to delay his enemies; after that he turned and burst at a run into the open street.

Out in the intersection fifty yards to his left, Seab Glazer had been alerted by the shot. If he had been content to stand his ground he would have made easy work of picking Holden off. Instead, in his eagerness, he started running even before he fired, and the bullet chopped into muddy ooze just behind the fugitive. Too late Glazer saw his mistake. Before he could plow to a halt, for better aim, Troy Holden had gained the other side of the street and plunged straight on into the alley.

Here a high board fence gave him momentary cover and he hugged it close as he sprinted over mud and cinders. To his left rose the rear walls of the business buildings that faced on Main Street; on the other hand were backyards and residences, mostly complete with fences and vegetable plots and chicken runs, woodsheds and privies. In one yard was a woman hanging clothes on a line, and a brindle dog on a chain that leaped and bayed in a thwarted frenzy to get at him.

He knew he had only seconds. Where a good-sized bush in new leaf grew beside a shed standing flush with the alley, he dropped into cover. Crouched there, with a shoulder against the rough boards and gun in hand, he almost at once heard hurried footsteps. Starke and Wasco came by at a jog trot. He wondered about Glazer, then guessed that he must be staying on the main street, beyond the row of business houses; these two were keeping pace with him, checking the slot between each pair of buildings to make sure their quarry didn't try to slip free by ducking into one of them. Confirming this, he watched the men pause briefly at the corner of the drygoods store opposite his hiding place, heard one of them shout something. Then they jogged on, out of sight, while he debated his next move.

As though to give him the answer, a shod hoof struck wooden flooring suddenly within the shed at his elbow. A horse! This was some townsman's private stable—and here was the chance, thrown in his lap, to saddle and take off across lots leaving his enemies vainly searching the town for him. But even as he came to his feet, something made him pause.

He thought, *By God, no!*

He had taken too much. He had been shot at, beaten, robbed, humiliated in every possible

131

way. He had lost everything he owned and even the girl he meant to marry. To lose his pride, now, by running away from these enemies would be the final defeat. Somehow he couldn't do it.

Yet a man who was no gunfighter had no business against a trio like those who were hunting him now. Troy Holden was afraid; it took a physical effort to keep from giving way to the muscular spasms that threatened to seize his whole body, and set his hands to trembling. He checked the loads of the Smith & Wesson—five bullets. Five shots, against the guns and the filled shell belts of three of Luke Bartell's killers . . .

Drawing a breath, he crossed to the rear of Fossen's drygoods store and up the three plank steps. The door was unlocked; he entered a dimly lit storeroom and groped his way forward, through a second door and past the curtained fitting room where he'd tried on his new clothes last evening. In the main room beyond, the merchant, Bert Fossen, and another man stood at the front window peering intently into the street. They turned as he came toward them along the aisle between counters piled high with yard goods and clothing.

The second man was By Peters; they both stared at Holden in a way that told they knew exactly what was going on—more than likely the whole town knew by now. Partly amused and partly irritated, he said, 'I hope nobody

132

minds my coming through the back way . . .'

The deputy sheriff found his tongue. 'Holden!' he exclaimed, and could get no further. Shouldering between the pair, Troy Holden started for the street door.

A strangled sound broke from the storekeeper. 'You're not going out there? Mister, this town's full of Bartell men—and they sound to me like they're after your hide!'

'Is that a fact?' he muttered sourly.

Even as he spoke, boots tramped the loose sidewalk boards outside. Seab Glazer appeared beyond the plate glass and halted there, his head turning restlessly. He had a baffled, angy look about him, as though the search was going badly and he failed to understand what could have become of his quarry. He lifted his gun, rubbed his jaw thoughtfully with the muzzle. And then Troy Holden sucked in his breath and held it, as he saw Glazer turn and look at the door beside him—almost as though some vagrant suspicion had crossed his mind. He actually put out a hand and laid it on the china knob.

The three within the store stood frozen, Holden himself falling into a crouch with the gun clutched tightly. Then, just as the knob began to turn, a cry sounded faintly somewhere down the street. Glazer's head whipped around. At once he whirled and was sprinting away, the warped boards carrying the thump of his running boots. And trapped breath whistled through the storekeeper's gaping jaws.

By Peters exclaimed softly, 'My God, I thought for a minute—'

'You thought what?' Troy Holden snapped. 'That there'd be a shooting, and you might have to do something about it? Well, you may still not be out of the woods! This thing isn't ended.'

The deputy raised a hand jerkily. Before he could manage a reply, Troy Holden was already striding to the door and wrenching it open.

Main Street lay entirely empty, but Holden felt certain the whole town was watching him from behind doors and windows. He tried to ignore this sensation as he waited, for long minutes, with his back pressed to the rough wall of the drygoods store and his eyes searching the street.

He could see no sign of the men he knew were hunting him. He switched the gun to his left hand while he rubbed the palm of his right along his pantleg. Then, feeling more alone and exposed to danger than he ever had, he started walking in the direction Seab Glazer had taken.

Staying close to the wall not only made him a less conspicuous target, but enabled him to raise less noise from the loose-laid planking. At each building corner he cautiously checked the alleyway beyond, before crossing to the next. By the time he had traveled a dozen yards, the sweat was flowing freely down his ribs.

Somewhere in the town, someone was working a pump with a squeaky handle; the rhythmic sound drifted across the stillness and presently stopped. In the livery, across the street, a horse whickered and went through a brief flurry of stomping, momentarily drawing Holden's attention and sharply tightening his nerves before he placed the sound.

Under the tin arcade fronting a harnessmaker's shop, a display of fancy saddles was racked either side of the open doorway. It was here that Holden suddenly caught the sound of a boot striking wood, behind him, and he halted and spun in midstride.

The towhead, Starke, was just stepping up onto the board-walk. Scarcely thinking, Holden went to one knee behind the rack that held one of those saddles; Starke fired in the same instant and lead chewed a sliver of wood from the window frame above his head. Holden dropped his forearm upon the saddle, bracing his wrist there; the smell of new, oiled leather mingled with exploding powder as he worked the trigger, aiming at a balloon of smoke from the gun in front of Starke's belt buckle. To the mingling of the shots, Starke jackknifed; bent double by the bullet's impact he stumbled back, struck an arcade support and went spiraling around it to land, rolling, in the mud of the street.

For a moment Troy Holden could do no more than stare at the first man he had ever killed.

He thought he had never seen such stillness as there was in the grotesque and terrible sprawl of that body—the head to one side, face pressed in the dirt; an arm bent crookedly under it, one spurred and booted leg canted across the edge of the walk. Slowly he straightened to his feet. And in the very next breath he was whirling to fade through the open door, into the dim interior of the harness shop.

The hurrying steps that had given him warning drew quickly nearer. Suddenly here was Seab Glazer with the breed, Wasco, at his heels. They halted by the body of Starke, breathing hard from their run; Glazer looked, and started to swear in a steady, monotonous undertone.

Troy Holden forced himself to step from the shadowed doorway. With all their attention on the dead man, the two seemed unaware of him and he was about to speak a challenge, when the sharp ears of the breed must have caught some sound. The man turned; smoky eyes, filled with a pure malevolence, met his and the man started to raise his gun.

Holden kept coming. The Smith & Wesson's barrel swept in a chopping arc against the side of the breed's skull. As the hat with the snakeskin band popped from his head, Wasco's eyelids fluttered and his knees broke and he dropped without a sound, and Holden's gun muzzle fell to point directly at Seab Glazer's chest.

'You can join them, if you want to,' Holden said bluntly. 'It's up to you!'

The redhead's chest swelled. For a moment, seeing the hatred in his narrow face, Holden didn't know what to expect; but then with a grimace Glazer dropped the gun into his holster and let his hand fall away from it. Between tight lips he said, 'You win this time, dude. But not again—not ever!'

The street, that had been empty and silent a moment before, was beginning to come to life. Doors slammed, men appeared but still hung back—perhaps they weren't convinced it was really over, and safe enough to satisfy their curiosity without danger of becoming involved. Now from the direction of the drygoods store came Fossen, the merchant, with By Peters' loose-hung shape towering over him. Holden nodded to them; he said coldly, 'A dead man for you, Sheriff. And a couple of prisoners, if you want them . . .'

'You're pushing your luck, Holden!' Seab Glazer grunted. He turned to the lawman then, and as their eyes met Holden saw By's face drain of color. 'What about it, Sheriff?' Glazer's words were coldly taunting. 'You want to try arresting me, maybe?'

By Peters looked at him; his stare touched on the redhead's holstered gun and slid hastily away again. A muscle at the corner of his mouth quirked, pulling his mouth out of shape; he wet his lips. Troy Holden could imagine the consuming longing for the brandy bottle in his desk drawer.

Obviously he was on the edge of panic. Just as obviously Glazer knew it.

The whole thing was all at once a farce and Troy Holden had had all he wanted. It was battle enough to avoid showing the aftermath of high tension that left him shaken. He kept his voice level as he said, 'So far as I'm concerned, I'm satisfied if they know now I'm not to be got rid of as easily as they might have been led to think.'

'Oh?' The redhead's eyes locked with his, in a look of mutual, naked hostility.

During this the breed, Wasco, had been recovering from the blow of Holden's gunbarrel. It had broken a crimson trickle of blood down the side of his face; Wasco had pushed to a sitting position but his head hung groggily forward. Now Seab Glazer leaned, hooked his friend under an arm and hauled him to his feet.

'Come on!' he grunted. 'Pull yourself together. We're riding.' He picked up the hat with the snakeskin band and jammed it on the breed's head, retrieved his gun and shoved it in the holster. He pointed the man toward the place where their horses stood.

Holden said sharply, 'Wait a minute!' He indicated the body of Starke. 'What about him?'

Briefly Glazer had turned back for a look at the dead man. He lifted his eyes to Holden and they were devoid of any feeling at all. 'You killed him,' he said. 'You can bury him!' But he was the one who broke gaze, and not a man there failed to notice it. With a shrug, he turned away; in dead silence, they watched him walk to his horse, give the unsteady Wasco a peremptory boost into the saddle, and mounting, take the reins of Starke's animal.

They rode north, toward the valley trail, with Wasco bobbing unsteadily over the saddlehorn, and the dead man's horse trailing. They neither one looked back.

CHAPTER FOURTEEN

For the next hour Troy Holden tried to empty his head of thought; since his problems appeared insoluble anyway, he put them out of his mind while he had a shave and used the tin bathtub in the barber shop's back room, and then went down the street for a meal at the restaurant. It was still short of midmorning when he stepped outside and saw a bunch of riders approaching.

There were Jim Ells, Morgan Peters and his foreman Ed Dewhurst, and another Kettle Creek cowman named Thacher. Something told Holden they were looking for him, even before they caught sight of him and with one accord reined over. From the saddle, Morgan Peters spoke. 'We want to see you, Holden.'

Still bothered by dark suspicions put in his head by Costello the saloonkeeper, Holden said shortly, 'Maybe I don't want to see you!'

He caught the quick hostility in Jim Ells' windwhipped face—even if he had saved Holden from a beating, yesterday, jealousy over Callie Peters would always be his overriding sentiment. Big Morgan Peters scowled and answered, in a tone of puzzlement, 'Holden, I don't get it! Yesterday, at my camp, you were looking for help from the Creek ranchers in the struggle with Luke Bartell. We're here, now, with what we thought you'd call good news. What's changed you?'

Troy Holden was in a mood to say that a great deal had happened to change him. But despite his almost sure conviction that one of these men had used the rifle that nearly killed him, something in the looks of them made him pause. Curiosity won out. He nodded shortly and said, 'All right. I was just going back to the hotel. Meet me there.'

Peters nodded, and the four pulled abruptly away.

Holden took his own time, following. When he passed the spot where Starke had died he tried not to look too closely; a dark stain of blood remained, though Deputy Sheriff Peters had had the body moved to the back room of the furniture store where a coffin was being nailed together for it, and someone else had tried to douse the boardwalk clean with a bucket of water.

However many times he might walk that street, Holden knew, he would think of it as the place where he had killed his first man.

The horses were tied before the hotel and their owners were waiting in the lobby when he got there. They had the dingy room to themselves, with its tacky furniture and wilted rubber plant; Morgan Peters began the talking, without preliminary: 'We thought you'd like to know things are stirring along the Creek—mainly because of you, Holden. Jim Ells, here, and Callie, started it when they brought us word of what happened to you, after you left my camp.'

Troy Holden nodded. 'I could have ended up in the same shape as poor Sam Riggs, except for Ells puttting a stop to it. A lucky break for me.'

'I tried to tell you,' the blond man said curtly, 'that it was Callie's doing I stepped in—or that I was even there. I got no reason to go out of my way to do you a favor. Or to look for trouble with Seab Glazer.'

Holden gave him a look. 'That's all right. You made it clear enough.'

Morgan Peters had waited out the interruption. 'You told Callie and Jim,' he went on, 'that Bartell admitted he has a thousand head of beef cattle heading for the valley. I understand you said they might even be reaching here sometime today.'

'According to Bartell. Yes.'

Peters drummed the arm of the sofa with rope-toughened fingers. 'Believe me, it puts a whole new complexion on things. Nobody's been anxious to make a fight with that outfit; but some of us ain't ready to stand by and let something like this happen, either. A thousand head of new cattle, suddenly dumped onto this range, could be a real threat.

'Of course, the first thing is to make sure the threat is real. If Bartell's bringing in a herd, I figure he'll cut across a corner of the Blackfeet Reservation and then straight south, up the creek. Accordingly I sent a rider, at first light, to do some scouting and report back.'

'Meanwhile,' Ed Dewhurst said, 'we're out going the rounds—seeing everybody. Thacher, here, has already thrown in with us; there'll be others. And their crews!'

'That's right,' Peters seconded his foreman. 'Naturally, there's some who try to argue that Luke's got a right to stock the ranch he bought from you, any way he sees fit. They don't want to face the proof that he stole Crown, and that he's out to steal the rest of this range the same way!'

Frowning, Holden looked at the tailormade cigarette he had taken from its box. He said

142

slowly, 'I'm wondering if Jim Ells, or Callie, remembered to tell you that I've lost the deed to Crown? Once Luke Bartell forges my name and registers transfer of title at the county seat, I won't have a thing to fight with!'

Morgan Peters leaned forward in his chair, to lay a forefinger on the other man's knee. 'One thing you ain't,' he said, 'is a quitter. That's why we came to you. And no sooner do we hit town,' he added, 'than my brother and a whole bunch of other people meet us with word of Bartell's men trying for you this morning— and you killing one, and sending the others packing. Damned if it didn't take you to show us it can be done!' The tall rancher wagged his head. 'No question, we need someone like that on our side. Throw in with us and maybe we can help get your deed and your ranch back for you.'

Holden looked at him sourly, not answering at once, remembering that this was the same man who once had scornfully given orders to stay away from his daughter. The man's attitude had changed since then—since yesterday, even, when Holden had got a turndown from him at the roundup camp. Now positions were reversed, and these men wanted his help.

He snapped a match and got the cigarette alight. And at that moment boots struck the veranda outside and a man who looked as though he had ridden hard came bursting into the lobby. As he looked hastily around, Morgan Peters lifted a hand and said, 'Over here, Charlie.' Charlie came ringing his spurs across the worn linoleum.

'I seen the broncs outside,' he exclaimed, a little breathless. 'Figured you must be here . . . Boss, Milt Spurrier came back from the reservation, hell for leather. I volunteered to bring you the word.'

'And that is?' the rancher prodded.

'There's a herd coming, all right. Milt used the glasses on 'em—figures not much less than a thousand head, and at least six riders pushing them. They're pointed straight for the creek.'

Excitement galvanized his hearers. Morgan Peters demanded, 'When will they hit it?'

'He thinks, sometime toward midafternoon.'

'Then there's time. We can stop them!'

'By God, yes!' Peters slapped both hands on his thighs and swung impetuously to his feet. 'We'll see whether Kettle Creek's to be had for the taking! We'll stop this herd and turn it back, before Bartell can so much as lay hands on it!'

Still seated, Holden peered up at the rancher through the smoke of his cigarette. 'You really think you have the men for the job?'

'The men, and the place! Squawhead, just above the rapids where the canyon narrows in. We can dig in there, if we have to—put in a stopper they can never get past, even were there twice the cattle and three times the crew to push them!'

Holden frowned thoughtfully. He knew the place and had to concede it could make a good defense—a tough granite spur, creating a bottleneck past which Kettle Creek forced its way in a boiling chain of cataracts and minor whitewater rapids. At the base of the spur, whose characteristic shape gave Squawhead its name, there were fallen boulders where armed men could hole up and do a job of fending off anyone trying to move up the canyon past them.

And yet something about this whole business seemed somehow, vaguely wrong, and trying to put a name to it kept Holden where he was while the rest of these men stood by waiting impatiently for his answer. Morgan Peters prodded him: 'Well? What about it, Holden? We'd admire to have you along.'

Then Jim Ells suggested, with a trace of a sneer, 'Maybe the affair this morning with them three Bartell riders was nothing but an accident. He's been talking a good fight against the ones that took his ranch away from him— but he don't appear to care much about getting into the show-down!'

That lifted Holden's head with a jerk. His eyes pinned the blond man's, as he got slowly to his feet. He said crisply, 'You can look for me at Squawhead. I have another piece of business I've got to attend to before I can join you—but don't worry: I'll join you.'

From Ells' look, he was pretty sure the blond

rancher only half believed him. Peters, however, appeared satisfied. The big man nodded. 'Good!' he said, and he turned across the dingy lobby, the others following. Holden watched them go tramping hurriedly outside to their waiting horses; after that, he turned toward the stairs and climbed quickly to his room.

He wanted to give those others time to leave town ahead of him, and so he took his time. Having checked the reloaded Smith & Wesson, and pocketed it together with what remained of the shells he'd bought from Yance Kegley, he delayed a little longer before picking his hat off the brass bedpost and walking back down through the hotel building. At the livery, across the intersection, he put the gear on his bay horse and led him outside—to discover Callie Peters in the saddle of her favorite pony, waiting for him.

She grinned as she saw his expression. 'I'll bet you didn't expect *me*.' But instantly she sobered. 'Are you all right, Troy? Oh, your face!'

He touched a swollen cheek. 'Still a little sore. But it's nothing really. Nothing for you to worry about.'

'How can I help but worry?' she began, but Holden was already lifting into the saddle, anxious to be off, and he scarcely heard her. Any other time he would have enjoyed a chance for her company; now, he simply could not afford it.

Fortunately, she appeared not to have heard of his shooting scrape with the Bartell riders, for she said nothing about it. Her mind was on other things. 'Have you any idea what Pa's up to?' she demanded, reining her pony closer. 'And Jim, and the others? I saw them riding out, just now, but they wouldn't tell me. They were in such a lather to be going—and now you, too. I *know* something's wrong!'

Holden looked at the appeal in her eyes. Her anxiety touched him, but he shook his head. 'I'm sorry.'

'Meaning, you know but you won't tell me, either!'

'I'm sorry,' he repeated. 'Right now I've got to be going.'

The girl's jaw settled. 'Go ahead, then. But you should know, from the old days, you don't get rid of me that easy. If you won't tell me what's happening I'll just tag along and find out!'

'Callie! No!' But then he sighed, recognizing an unbeatable stubborn streak in her; he shrugged. 'If I were your father I could warm your britches and send you home. Since you're too big for that, I suppose it's hopeless!' Instantly she was grinning again, and she put her horse alongside his as he kicked the bay into motion down the muddy, puddled street.

'Where are we going?'

He was too angry with her to answer.

147

*   *   *

A thin pencil line of smoke rose from Yance Kegley's mud-and-slab stovepipe chimney, and the old man's horse was in the corral, but at first Holden could see nothing of the hermit himself. He hailed the shack but got no answer. Since it was close to noon, he reasoned Kegley must be somewhere close. Callie Peters stayed in the saddle, watching in silence as he stepped down and stood looking around and slapping the reins into his palm impatiently.

He could feel the pressure of time, and also the nagging ache of the healed bullet wound in his back, aggravated now by hours of steady riding; both horses were heated and blowing, from the stiff pace he'd set over the hill trails . . .

Then Yance Kegley came in sight through the scrub pine, following the path from the spring with a bucket of water at the end of one arm and throwing that bad leg in his limping gait. The old man set his pail down. He eyed the marks on Holden's face and said, 'Well! What happened to you? Looks like you ran into trouble, after you left yesterday. I could have told you!'

Holden admitted it with a nod. 'And there's more on the way.'

'Bartell?'

He nodded again. 'I was hoping you could

148

help.'

'Me?' Kegley looked narrowly from one to the other of his visitors. 'I somehow didn't think the two of you had dropped in for dinner ... What is it you want from me this time?'

'Something I remember seeing in the shed. Come along and I'll fill you in.'

Callie wasn't included in the invitation. Troy Holden was still put out with her, for insisting on coming after he had asked her not to; but stronger than this emotion, he realized, was one of concern over what might happen to her. Somehow he had never understood that he could feel quite so protective toward this girl whom he'd almost watched grow up, during the intervals of their acquaintance.

Now he left her with the horses and he and Yance Kegley walked over to the shed, Holden explaining in a few words what was building between Bartell and the valley ranchers, and what he had in mind. The old wolfer listened with scowling intentness, finally nodding. 'It might be something to see!' he admitted, beginning to show his yellowed teeth in a wicked grin. 'Hell, yes! But—you ever used this stuff?'

'No.'

'I thought likely. Then you'll need a hand with it.' Kegley pawed at the beard stubble that bristled his jaws, and nodded as he reached a decision. 'Reckon I'll just throw leather on my bronc and ride along with you. Don't worry—I won't hold you up none. And I got an idea this is something I wouldn't want to miss . . .'

Shortly they were in the saddle and making for the valley floor again, at the point where Kettle Creek broke through the narrow gap at Squawhead. Despite his bad leg, Kegley was no mean horseman and he knew every deer trail and shortcut. But as they rode, munching cold meat sandwiches the old man had prepared, Troy Holden watched the movement of the sun overhead and worried about the inexorably passing time.

The long detour by way of Kegley's shack had eaten up more of the day than he had anticipated. More and more he began to wonder if they could hope to reach their goal before real trouble hit.

And when a shift of wind into their faces brought the faint rattling of gunfire, somewhere ahead, he knew he had failed and that they were too late.

CHAPTER FIFTEEN

A hand caught at Holden's sleeve. Callie Peters' face tilted anxiously toward his. 'That's Pa, isn't it?' Her voice broke. 'What's he up to? You've *got* to tell me now!'

'It sounds as though he's up to his ears in trouble,' Holden answered shortly, jerking free.

'We'll find out soon enough.' Yance Kegley was pushing unerringly ahead. With the others close behind, he led the way along a steep ridge where they had to double forward in their saddles to avoid the low-growing pine branches, then into a ravine and up across the adjoining ridge. Here a sharp twist to the right plunged them into a descending draw that was choked with brush and scrub growth.

It was treacherous work and the horses were tiring fast. They went down in single file, fighting not to overrun one another, the riders praying against missed footing in the treacherous spill of rubble. And abruptly they dropped out of the timber, and there was a view of what lay below.

Kettle Creek came flashing and tumbling in white water through the narrows of Squawhead, with scarcely enough level room on its far bank to contain the wagon road. Below the narrows, the canyon walls funneled out again; and it was here the Kettle Creek ranchers led by Morgan Peters had taken their position, in talus that skirted the base of Squawhead spur. So situated, they could have turned back any herd, or even a small army if one had tried to move past them. Anyone could see at a glance that Callie's father had used sound strategy.

But good as it was, it had failed him. Those boulders were little protection from the guns that had been planted on the timbered flank of the spur itself. Now the guns were taking a toll; what should have been an easy victory for the Kettle Creek men had been turned into a furious and nearly one-sided battle. Seeing how badly they were pinned down, listening to the confused mingling of six-gun and rifle fire, Troy Holden could only groan as he recognized at last the thought that had been gnawing and troubling him all along.

He said in bitter self-accusation, 'Damn it, I should have seen Luke Bartell was only spreading bait, when he let me know he had a herd coming! He was counting on me to pass the news. He knew if Morgan Peters decided on an effort to turn them back, this would have to be the spot. By placing his own guns on the ridge, he'd have them like sitting ducks!'

Yance Kegley said suddenly, 'Look yonder . . .'

Downstream, the burnished smear of sunlight on creek surface caused a man to squint; but Holden could see now the strung-out formation of the trail cattle, coming slowly up the far bank. The riders didn't seem to be pushing them hard; probably their instructions were to hang back until Bartell had a way cleared. The cattle, moving easily and almost under their own momentum, were still a good many minutes away.

An anguished cry broke from Callie Peters, and brought Holden's eyes to her to see the tears upon her face. 'Can't we do anything?'

'If we do it will have to be quick!' he answered bluntly. 'Dug in where he is, there's no chance in the world of getting Bartell—but just possibly he can be drawn off.' He turned to Kegley. 'I'm going to ask you to see that this girl stays right here out of trouble. Don't let her do anything foolish.'

'Oh, hell!' The old man shook his shaggy head. 'Let her look out for her own self! I come this far, Holden—I'm gonna be in at the end. I got my reasons.' And he kicked his horse and started it on down the draw. Holden appealed to the girl with an exasperated look; but there was no time to reason with her and, turning away, he sent the bay plummeting in the old man's wake.

They came down onto level ground without a spill and spurred ahead, pushing the tired horses to the limit. Where Kettle Creek slowed down again below the rapids, they hit the water in a high, reckless splashing. Pulling out under the farther bank, they were conscious of the sporadic working of guns at the narrows; but now, also, above the murmur of the water they could hear a first rumbling of the approaching herd.

Yance Kegley opened the gunnysack he had carried tied to his saddlehorn and brought out the dynamite sticks, already capped and fused. 'You light 'em, count two, and throw—*hard*! If you count three, no use to bother about throwing . . .'

Gingerly, Holden put one stick in his coat pocket and dug out a match, holding it ready as they rode forward at a walk toward the approaching herd. Presently he said, 'Close enough!' and they both pulled rein.

Holden popped the match on a thumbnail. He held it while they lighted their fuses, and then let the match fall and stood in stirrups listening to Kegley count aloud in a voice that was high-pitched with excitement. They threw precisely together; the sticks lobbed end for end, trailing sparks, and struck the earth well ahead of the point animals. And instinctively both men ducked their heads between their shoulders, as red fire and powder blast seemed to rip the canyon apart.

The ground shook mightily; the horses squealed and reared. Stunned by shock waves, Holden brought the bay under control and peered into a screen of smoke as debris began to patter down around him. The massive sound pulsed and rolled away between the shouldering ridges, and his numbed ears began to be aware of other things—the sudden bawling of terrified cattle, the rumble of hooves lunging into motion.

If gunfire still raged behind them at the narrows, he no longer heard it. He caught sight of Yance Kegley and swung his arm forward, shouting, 'Keep after it!'

They rode into the smoke, picking their way among debris and past the crater the dynamite had blasted. Holden dug the second stick from his pocket, with a hand that shook. The smoke pall began to shred out; he saw what had become a tangled mass of cattle trying to turn on itself and break into a stampede, heard terror in the sounds lifting from hundreds of throats. If stopping the herd had been the one purpose, they had already accomplished it; but Holden wasn't satisfied. He pulled close beside Kegley and yelled above the uproar, 'Let's give them another round—just in case Bartell didn't hear that one!'

Again the fuses were lighted, the sticks went arcing, and Holden pulled in behind a solitary pine for such protection as it could give when the blast struck. Kegley had thrown harder and farther than his companion; Holden distinctly saw one dark form hurled high, grotesquely spinning. And now real, blind panic hit the herd and tore it apart, to plunge headlong into the waters of the creek or scatter senselessly across the open flats. Ears still ringing, blinded by smoke and powder flash, Holden heard a horse scream shrilly and cringed at the thought of a rider going down before that tide of hooves and meat and horns.

A little sickened, he turned back. He had lost Yance Kegley in the confusion and the drifting smoke; meanwhile, it seemed to him the racket of gunplay had ceased, yonder at the narrows. He took the Smith & Wesson from his pocket and held it in his lap as he kicked the

155

bay in that direction, to find out if his strategy with the dynamite had paid off the way he hoped. He was vaguely aware that shooting had broken out again at the narrows.

Suddenly he was aware of a drum of running horses, dead ahead and drawing nearer. Two riders came bursting around a point of rock and timber, and they were Bartell and Glazer; as they saw him in the middle of the road, they hauled in so sharply that Seab Glazer's nervous mount danced about under him in a complete circle. Luke Bartell shouted, 'By God, Holden, is this your doing?'

'Every bit of it!' Holden answered. 'You won't turn that stampede this side of Canada!' And in spite of the odds there was all at once no fear in him at all—only the exultation of facing his enemy, and knowing that he had finally managed to hit the man where it hurt.

For now Bartell was cursing him, his face distorted with black fury. And in the next breath a gun rose in his hand and the outlaw fired, point blank.

The saddle of a nervous horse was a poor base for shooting. The bullet came nowhere near close; neither did the one that Holden fired hurriedly, in reply. Seab Glazer, he saw, had a gun and was trying to get a shot at him, but Bartell's horse backed into his and for that moment the redhead had all he could do to settle it. The leader, cursing foully, leveled for another shot.

A rifle spoke, somewhere at Holden's right. Bartell's whole body shook to the impact of a bullet. His head jerked forward, the reins slipped from his hand. As the outlaw started to double forward, Troy Holden twisted for a look.

He had known the rifleman must be Yance Kegley, even before he heard the old man's yell of triumph and saw the unholy glee on his face. With a smoothly practiced move Kegley flipped the rifle, to crank the lever, and dropped its barrel across his forearm again, hunting for Seab Glazer. In the same instant Glazer fired. The slug struck old Kegley square; it sent the rifle flying from his grasp as it picked him off his saddle. He slammed to the ground and his momentum carried him, rolling, over the edge of the cutbank and down the sharp drop to the creek.

Then Troy Holden, taking careful aim down the whole length of his arm, brought the redhead into his sights and worked the trigger, and somehow knew the shot was good even as a burst of powdersmoke blurred his vision.

In the shocked aftermath of the mingled weapons, he realized he was the only one left in a saddle, still unhurt. Slowly he lowered his gun, too numbed for the moment to do more than look at the crumpled figures of Bartell and Glazer lying in the road. Seab Glazer's frenzied horse, out of its head with panic, spun wildly and one hoof struck its owner's body,

157

causing it to give limply. Then the animal went galloping away, reins and stirrups flopping.

The other horses had already begun to settle. Troy Holden took a long breath, filling his lungs with the stink of burnt powder, and reined over to look at Yance Kegley.

Kegley sprawled at the creek's edge, an arm and part of his torso bobbing in the water. Holden stepped hurriedly from saddle, keeping hold of the reins as he took the shallow drop sliding on his heels. Crouched there, the sound of a galloping horse made him freeze and lift his gun as a Bartell rider swept suddenly into view.

The man was bareheaded, bent forward in the saddle and frantically whipping up his horse with the ends of the reins. Holden saw him discover the bodies of his dead leaders; he didn't even pause to look at them. A sidelong, almost indifferent glance flicked over Holden, in passing, and then the man was gone.

And Troy Holden deliberately lowered the hammer of the gun and dropped it into his coat pocket, having seen enough to convince him he no longer needed it.

Yance Kegley's blood was beginning to stain the water of the creek. Holden went down on one knee and pulled the man up onto the bank, and propped his head at a better angle. His mouth tightened as he saw the hole Glazer's bullet had drilled in the old man's chest.

Kegley stirred. His eyes came open and

discovered Holden bending over him. He tried and found speech: 'Bartell?'

'He's dead. You killed him.'

'So!' The word was a grunt of satisfaction. 'So this time I made it!'

'This time?' Troy Holden echoed, and suddenly had a premonition of what he was about to hear.

The old man actually tried to laugh shortly, but it ended in a cough and a grimace of pain. 'Hell!' he muttered. 'It was him I was trying for, the night I put that bullet in your back . . .'

'*You?*'

'You never guessed, did you? And damned if I was going to admit I'd made such a damned fool mistake. But you had to come along the trail just the wrong time, that night. I thought you was Luke Bartell—and there I'd been waiting, a dozen years, to even my score with him!

'You ever wonder,' he demanded, forcing the words from a chest wracked by contractions of pain, 'where I got this gimp leg of mine? It was down at Billings—twelve years ago. I drove the wagon in from my homestead ranch, one day, just as Bartell and a gang hit the bank and got driven off empty handed. Bartell was killing mad, shooting at everything in sight. He seen me on the wagon seat. He couldn't help but see I didn't have no gun, but that never stopped him. For pure devilment he threw a bullet at me as he went past. It took me in the hip, knocked me off the wagon. The leg never healed right. By time I got out of the hospital I'd lost my ranch, lost everything. Couldn't even hold a riding job. And all these years since, I just been bidin' my time—waiting . . .'

Sweat stood in huge drops on the old man's leathery face. 'That night in the Montana House, Bartell looked straight in my face and I was sure he remembered me. Later I heard somebody behind me on the road and I thought he'd followed me, to finish me off before I could finish him. Wasn't till after I'd shot that I seen my mistake. Wasn't nothing I could do then, but fetch you home and try to—'

The tortured words broke off in a last spasm. Yance Kegley fought for breath. A hand caught at Holden's sleeve and tightened on it, a shaking grip. Then the blood poured from his mouth and he fell back limp, and Holden let him down.

Shaking, he could only stare at the dead man who—he knew now, beyond any question—must have been deranged from years of pain, and loneliness, and a festering hatred for the one who had crippled him. Only a crazy man would have thought that Bartell would remember him, a dozen years later—after a single glance, and a casual shooting. Or that, even having recognized him, Luke Bartell would have been bothered about completing the job.

Only a crazy man would have left Holden in

160

the dark about the ambush, letting him read all kinds of meaning into what had been, after all, no more than a simple accident . . .

More riders approaching brought him quickly to his feet then, to see Morgan Peters, and Callie beside him. Not until now did he realize that all the shooting had stopped; with Bartell's cattle stampeded down the valley, out of sight and hearing, a strange silence lay upon the land. He could hear the lapping of Kettle Creek, a twittering of birds flitting through the new-leafed brush along the bank.

Callie and her father reined in, to stare at the bodies of the dead men. Then Callie slipped from the saddle and came running to Holden; her face was white and her voice tremulous as she cried: 'Troy! You're not hurt? Oh, please don't be!'

'None at all,' he assured her, and saw relief flood warm color into her cheeks. She was in his arms, then, her face against his chest, and almost of their own volition his arms closed about her and it seemed entirely natural she should be there. All at once it was as though Bea Applegate was someone he had known in some other world—someone whose face he could not even clearly remember.

He lifted his eyes to find Morgan Peters staring at the two of them, with an unreadable expression. 'So it's like that, is it?'

'I'm afraid it is,' Holden said; his words were mild but his answering look held defiance.

'Whether you like it or not, Morgan.'

'Uh-huh.' The rancher shifted his weight in the saddle and pushed the back of a hand across his mouth. When he spoke again his voice was gruff but it didn't sound really angry. 'Jim Ells is the one who ain't going to like it! Still, Jim's a reasonable man—when he sees he's got no choice but to be. Besides, even he has to admit that you pulled the lot of us out of a real bad hole, today.' The gaunt head nodded solemnly. 'Callie tells me using the dynamite was your idea. Man, man! You could have blown yourself to pieces!'

'But I didn't.'

'No. And it worked! When Bartell pulled his men down off the ridge to see what the hell was happening to his cattle, we were able to catch them on the flank. Only a few got away. Luke Bartell was one.' He looked at the bodies of the outlaws. 'I see he didn't get past you.'

'It was Yance Kegley that killed him,' Holden said quickly, for the record. He added, 'What about yourself? Did you lose any men?'

'One of my boys is dead, a couple wounded. Bob Thatcher took a bad one in the arm, but he'll recover. Thanks to you, it was no worse than that.' Peters was grinning suddenly. 'You ought to see Sam Riggs! He got that breed— that Wasco, that beat him up so bad. I think it done him good. He's holding his head up again—as if he'd suddenly took a new lease on life!'

His arm around Callie, Holden said, 'Tell Sam I'm going to want to talk to him. If he'd like a job at Crown, there'll be one waiting.'

Peters looked at him keenly. 'What does that mean? Sounds to me you're saying you aim to take Crown over—to run it.' And at Holden's nod: 'You're *not* going to sell?'

'A lot of things can happen,' Troy Holden said. 'A man can change. Something you've fought for can suddenly appear a lot more valuable than you ever knew.

'Somehow, it never occurred to me that I could come to think of myself as a part of this valley, or this Montana country. Now all at once I don't want to belong anywhere else.'

The rancher gave him a probing look; slowly he nodded; and there was satisfaction in the way he answered, 'I'm glad to hear that. Damned glad! I used to think Vern Holden had missed the big chance of his life, when he failed to realize just how much this country had to offer—besides a mere business investment. But maybe his son has found out in time. I hope so. I'd be glad to have you for a neighbor.'

'Perhaps something more than a neighbor,' Troy Holden said, and his arm tightened about the girl. Suddenly he felt not only frightened of the mistakes he had nearly made, but humbly grateful too. True, he had lost much; but he began to suspect he had gained infinitely more.

We hope you have enjoyed this Large Print book. Other Chivers Press or G.K. Hall & Co. Large Print books are available at your library or directly from the publishers.

For more information about current and forthcoming titles, please call or write, without obligation, to:

Chivers Press Limited
Windsor Bridge Road
Bath BA2 3AX
England
Tel. (01225) 335336

OR

G.K. Hall & Co.
P.O. Box 159
Thorndike, Maine 04986
USA
Tel. (800) 223-2336

All our Large Print titles are designed for easy reading, and all our books are made to last.